GUARDED BY THE HERO

HEROES OF FREEDOM RIDGE

MANDI BLAKE

Guarded by the Hero
Heroes of Freedom Ridge Book 7
Copyright © 2021 Mandi Blake
All Rights Reserved

Published in the United States of America
Cover Designer: Amanda Walker PA & Design Services
Editor: Editing Done Write
Ebook ISBN: 978-1-953372-12-3
Paperback ISBN: 978-1-953372-15-4

To Ginny and Tanya.
Thank you for believing in me first.

Above all else, guard your heart,
for everything you do flows from it.
Proverbs 4:23 (NIV)

CONTENTS

1

HEATH

*H*eath lowered the pistol in his hands and turned to Jeremiah, giving him a thumbs up.

Jeremiah jerked his head toward the exit, and Heath followed his business partner out of the indoor firing range and into the Freedom Tactical Firearms shop.

Heath removed his ear protection and safety glasses. "I think this is the one."

Jeremiah reached for the pistol and turned it over in his hands. "It's a good weight." He adjusted his hand on the grip before handing the firearm back to Heath. They had similar training and often shared weapon preferences. "I'll have to test this one out next time. I need to run if I'm going to see Miah before bed. It's a school night."

Heath accepted the firearm from his business partner and holstered it. He'd been eying the piece for weeks, and he was about to take the leap and get the new weapon. "Tell Shrimp I said her feet smell." Heath never missed a chance to play around with Miah. Jeremiah's daughter was at the fun age when she liked to tease and be teased.

"No way. She'll get all riled up and pester me until I call you so she can tell you off."

Heath laughed. "That's the fun part."

"Not when Haven wants her calming down for bedtime. I may tell her first thing in the morning so you can get that bossy wakeup call."

"Bring it on. See you tomorrow."

Adam walked in and greeted Jeremiah on his way out. Heath, Adam, and Jeremiah worked together at Got Your Six Security, but they usually met every other week after work for firearms training.

With three decades of military training between them, target practice was more for sport than honing the skill. Thankfully, personal security agents rarely needed firearm intervention. Their job serving as bodyguards was to protect and shield, not retaliate.

Adam greeted Heath with a fist bump. "You heading out too?"

"Nah, Jeremiah just had to get Miah to bed."

Heath jerked his chin toward the exit. "I'll hang around for a little bit."

"Ready for a round?" Adam asked.

"Always." Heath adjusted his headphones and glasses before heading back into the range and readying his stance.

"Winner takes all?" Adam yelled to be heard above the shots and through the noise-canceling headphones.

Heath nodded once and raised the pistol to eye level. His focus was sharp and accurate as the targets moved on rails around the room. One after the other, his shot found its mark. It had taken him years to adopt this self-assured attitude toward firearms, and training had become relaxing and therapeutic.

Heath was on a roll when a flash of movement waved across the periphery of his vision. Adam was signaling that he had something to say.

Heath stepped out of the range and back into the shop.

Adam pulled his headphones down to rest around his neck. "Dude, that thing is wicked."

Heath handed over the new pistol. "Try it out."

A range employee joined them and started answering Adam's questions about the 9mm, and Heath pulled his phone from the cargo pocket of his pants.

One voicemail from Mr. Hawkins and two texts

from his sister, Tessa. Heath listened to the voice-mail and stepped away from Adam and the employee to return the call.

Mr. Hawkins answered on the second ring. "You working late?" the older man asked in greeting. He'd been one of Heath's biggest clients at Got Your Six Security since the beginning.

Heath pulled his Bluetooth earpiece out of his pocket and connected it. "Always working. Tell me about the New Hope Gala."

"I sent you the specs in an email. I really just wanted to catch up."

Heath pulled up the email and scanned. The event would be massive, and Heath wanted the security contract. Mr. Hawkins talked as if Got Your Six already had the job. "How's the fam?" Heath asked.

"Driving me crazy. My youngest granddaughter wants a car for her birthday, but that child is the worst driver I've seen in my seventy years."

Heath chuckled. "Give her time, and maybe stay off the roads when you know she's out."

"She'll be the death of me. I know it."

"I'm reading your email. Tell me what you're looking for at the gala."

"I want a lot of feet on the ground, but I don't want an army. I don't want a bunch of barrel-chested men intimidating the donors."

Mr. Hawkins was a no-nonsense kind of guy, and

Heath appreciated that quality. It made his job easier.

"Yes, sir. I'm putting my partner in charge of this event. I just sent you the specs on Jeremiah Gilbert. You met him last May in Albuquerque. He's your man."

"I'll check it out. I remember Mr. Gilbert."

Heath leaned back against a wall between the shop and range. "Ten years in the Army, a few more as in-house security for NeoGene, and he was with the local PD before he came to Got Your Six full time. He's my partner for a reason."

"Can you spare a few men for live video surveillance?" Mr. Hawkins asked.

Heath typed the note into New Hope's file on his phone. "I'll make sure Jeremiah factors that in when he's putting together the team."

"You can email me the quote. Tomorrow. It's after seven in the evening where you are, son."

"Yes, sir," Heath said as he shot off a message to Jeremiah. "You'll have it in the morning."

"I appreciate it. We should get together once this is over. You play golf?" Mr. Hawkins asked.

Heath and the owner of the New Hope Foundation had gotten to know each other well over the course of planning the charity's last few high-profile events, but they lived on opposite sides of the States.

"I can't say I do, sir. Freedom's courses were buried beneath snow nine months of the year."

Mr. Hawkins chuckled. "A smart man knows his strengths and weaknesses."

"How do you feel about deep-sea fishing?" Heath asked.

"Now you're talkin'," Mr. Hawkins shouted. The man's raspy voice was always booming, but it was more friendly than assertive.

"I'll charter a boat for January. Have your assistant send me some dates when we can sneak off to the coast for a few days."

"Sure thing, son."

Heath touched the button on his earpiece to disconnect the call and made a note to send the quote in the morning. With so many wealthy investors, Mr. Hawkins spared no expense when it came to security at his charity events.

They'd met at the Freedom Ridge Resort last December when Mr. Hawkins visited with his family. Heath had been the head of security at the resort then, and he'd run into the retired millionaire by happenstance. Within two weeks, the two had bonded over their shared history with the United States Marine Corps.

Heath's career path had always been predestined. He came from a long line of Marines, and he'd stepped up and into his place. He hadn't let anything stand in his way until he accomplished that goal.

Too bad his life-long career ended too soon. He hadn't planned for civilian life, at least not before his fifties. Yet, the merge into security had been as close to seamless as he could have hoped. He was still able to do what he loved, but his days in a permanent office looked a lot different from the temporary bases he'd constructed with the Marines.

Heath checked the time on his watch. It was 19:47, and he knew better than to call Jeremiah tonight.

Heath's phone rang in his hand, and Tessa's name lit up the screen along with a photo. She had her arm slung over his shoulders, and her tongue stuck out one side of her mouth.

He pressed the button on his Bluetooth to answer the call. "Hey, sis."

"Dinner?" Tessa asked.

There was a lilt in her tone at the end of the word that implied a question, but it was clear she expected him to say yes. Fortunately, he had three strong sisters who knew what they wanted and knew how to get it.

At the mention of food, Heath's stomach let out a rumble. He'd forgotten to eat dinner. "Where?"

"Valentino's. Hold on a sec." Tessa's voice was

muffled as if she'd pulled the phone away from her face as she asked, "You like pizza?"

"Are you with someone?" Heath questioned.

Of course she was with someone. Tessa was everyone's best friend.

"My friend, Claire. She's eating with us."

"Where are you?" Heath asked. "Do I need to pick you up?"

"No, we'll walk. We just got out of our stained glass class at the civic center. I have *got* to show you my lantern! I'm entering it in the art display at the Tree Lighting Ceremony tomorrow."

"That's awesome. Can't wait to see it." Heath could hear a muffled voice in the background on Tessa's end of the call.

"See you in a jiffy."

"Be there lickety-split," Heath replied.

He'd been nine years old when his youngest sister was born, and they'd always had an unlikely bond centered around Tessa's quirky personality. "Normal" was not a word in Tessa's vocabulary.

When he disconnected the call, he joined Adam in the shop. "Hey, I'm gonna run. See you in the morning."

"You got it, Boss."

Before meeting his sister, Heath stopped by the security headquarters and checked the off-site security footage for any alerts and made his rounds through the small office locking up. He'd probably be back after dinner, but he never left an easy entry at the office. He housed too much sensitive information to be negligent.

Got Your Six Security had become his driving force since well before he actually opened the doors. Heath never did anything halfway, and security had been his life since he'd established a career in communication with the Marines.

There were certain parts of his life where complete control was necessary—the business, his finances, and awareness of his surroundings. He'd put too much into the security firm to accept anything but success, and he intended to work hard to see it thrive.

The constant mental push reminded him a lot of boot camp. Not because it was physically demanding, but because he was always looking for the smartest avenue. He was competing with himself. Be better today than yesterday. Push harder. Work smarter. Get through this trial so you can get through the next one.

He stepped out onto the dimly lit sidewalk along Jefferson Avenue and looked both ways before turning to lock the door and engage the alarm.

The cool mountain air hit the bare skin of his neck and sent a chill down his spine. Maybe getting his business off the ground wasn't so much like boot camp after all. San Diego had been sixty degrees hotter than the Colorado Rockies, and no one was shouting orders at him here.

Ten minutes later, he parked in the small lot on 2nd Street. Valentino's was directly across from the courthouse and was notorious for limited parking. Thankfully, there were only a few vehicles still dotting the street this late in the evening.

A faint dusting of snow covered the Freedom square in a white sheet. Preparations for the Tree Lighting Ceremony were underway. Food carts were pulling in, volunteers stood on ladders to check the myriad of colorful lights around the square, and half a dozen builders erected a temporary stage in front of the courthouse.

Heath stepped out onto the sidewalk and slowly scanned his surroundings. It was difficult to differentiate one thing from another when everything was white on white, but it wasn't as bad as the tan on tan of the Middle East. Even back home in Freedom, he took his time, noting every face and every shop that still had their interior lit.

He spotted Tessa and her friend at the corner of the next block and headed toward them. They were facing each other talking, and he took the moment before they spotted him to observe the interaction.

His sister sported her usual friendly smile, but her friend, Claire, looked troubled. She wore an oversized gray coat and heavy boots that were more functional than fashionable. Her brown hair was pulled back in a low ponytail that hung over one shoulder and disappeared into the collar of her coat.

As he got closer, he noticed Claire was frowning. A deep crease was etched on her forehead just above the bridge of her glasses.

"Come on. I promise you'll have fun," Tessa prodded.

"I don't know," Claire began. "I really should—"

Her head whipped toward him, slinging her ponytail into an arc behind her. She took two steps away from Heath and hunched her shoulders forward, tucking her arms around her middle.

The look of terror on her face stopped Heath in his tracks, and he held up his hands in surrender.

Good grief, the woman looked like a cornered animal. "Sorry, I didn't mean to sneak up on you."

"Heath!" Tessa squealed as she wrapped her arms around his shoulders. She was a good foot shorter than him, but her personality was big enough to make up for what she lacked in height. No one would make the mistake of overlooking Tessa Mitchell.

Except Heath wasn't concerned with his sister right now. Claire had loosened the tension in her shoulders, and the fearful look on her face was beginning to dissipate.

She was definitely a natural beauty. With her hair pulled back, he could clearly see the outline of her heart-shaped face, though her pointed chin stayed tucked close to her chest. He'd barely gotten a look at her eyes before her attention moved to the ground, then left and right. She looked everywhere except at him.

Heath made a point of assessing everyone he met. You could tell a lot about someone by their handshake, clothes, reactions, and body language. Unfortunately, the label on this package didn't reveal what was inside.

Tessa released him from her bubbly greeting hug and grabbed Claire's hand. "This is Claire. She's a little shy, but I told her you're just a big teddy bear. Nothing to be afraid of."

The fact that his sister had needed to assure Claire that he wasn't anyone to fear before they'd even met set off a few alarms in Heath's brain. Everything about her expression and posture said to tread carefully. She looked like she'd spook faster than a deer in open season.

"Heath Mitchell." He extended his hand to her, fully prepared to be left hanging judging from her initial wariness.

He waited one extra second before she slid her hand from where it had been smothered by her coat and tentatively grasped his. "Claire Odom."

Her hand was warm and soft like her voice. She pulled it away before the actual shake, only making contact with his skin for a split-second, if that.

Tessa bounced on her toes and gave a cheerleader clap. "Now that we all know each other, we can eat!"

Heath gestured for Claire and his sister to lead the way, and Claire seemed to have a hard time keeping her gaze on the sidewalk ahead of her.

He wasn't sure what to think of Claire's unease, but as she cast a glance at him over her shoulder, he knew it wasn't him she was afraid of.

2

CLAIRE

*C*laire inhaled the cold, dry air and clung to Tessa's hand. The hair on her head felt as if each strand was standing on end.

"Relax," Tessa leaned closer to whisper. "Heath is here. You're fine."

Claire didn't know Heath from Adam's house cat, and his presence on the sidewalk behind her didn't assure her of her safety. If anything, an extra shot of adrenaline rushed through her veins.

"I told you he's in security. Like a bodyguard," Tessa said. "He's the best."

Claire could admit that Heath *sounded* like the best, judging from the way Tessa talked about him, but it had been a long time since she'd ventured out in such a public place after dark. She squeezed her eyes closed and murmured through gritted teeth, "I don't know if I can do this."

Tessa stopped and lifted Claire's hand, holding it between both of hers. "I believe you can do this, but if you think you can't, I can walk you back to your car."

Claire silently repeated her mantra. *This isn't Savannah, and I'm okay.*

When she opened her eyes, they were standing in front of Valentino's, a local pizza place that Tessa raved about. Claire hadn't tried the food herself, but Tessa could sell water to a fish, and she'd somehow convinced Claire to venture *way* out of her comfort zone and go out for dinner after their stained glass class.

Even the art class was out of her comfort zone. She'd spent six years pursuing a rigorous art degree, but those days felt like a forgotten dream. She'd left Georgia four years ago without that piece of paper.

It was tragic how one event had changed her forever, leaving her with scars and enough emotional trauma that her therapist hadn't been able to touch it.

Tessa squeezed Claire's hand. "Your call."

Heath stopped beside them but kept a healthy distance that she appreciated.

"Everything okay?" he asked. One of his brows

lifted slightly, changing the hard edges of his face into a softer expression.

"Yes," Claire said. "Let's go."

She kept a firm grip on Tessa's hand as they stepped into the restaurant. The lights were dim, and shadows fell across several burgundy and tangerine walls. The warm smell of parmesan and oregano filled her nose, and she recalled long-forgotten memories of her older neighbor as a child who'd let her help roll out the pizza dough on her laminate kitchen counter.

The nostalgia of the scent and Tessa's presence gave Claire the courage to follow her friend to an empty booth in the back. She slid onto the bench seat and relaxed as Tessa sat beside her. Heath took the seat across from them.

Claire had triggers. Dark streets were one of them, while small-town pizza joints were not.

"I'm starving," Tessa drawled. "What are you getting?"

Claire looked up to see that Tessa's question was directed toward her. "Um, I think maybe pepperoni and black olives."

Tessa scrunched up her thin nose. "I was hoping we could share, but I'll have to pass on black olives."

"I'll split a pizza with you," Heath said.

Claire lifted her gaze from the worn table to

Heath's soft brown eyes. She quickly looked back to the menu. "Thanks."

"Heath will eat almost anything," Tessa said, relaxing against the booth at her back.

Heath's grin was slightly pulled to one side, revealing straight, white teeth. "You spend three months eating MREs in Kandahar and you take what you can get."

Tessa held up a hand. "No, thanks. I'll stick to pizza and pasta."

A middle-aged waitress stepped up to their table and flipped to a blank page in her pad. "What can I get for you this evening?"

Tessa sat up straighter, only gaining an inch of height. "I'll have a medium Rome is for Lovers, deep dish, with a root beer."

When Claire looked at Heath, he was looking back at her. He nodded once, indicating she should order.

"We'll be sharing a large pepperoni and black olive pizza."

"Drink?" the waitress prompted.

"Water."

Heath handed the menus to the waitress with a friendly smile. "Water for me, too."

When the waitress left, Heath rested his arms on the table. "So, you're taking a stained glass class?"

Tessa slapped her palm against the table. "Yes!

And we're rockin' it." She tipped a finger toward Claire. "Tell him how awesome we are."

Claire's eyes widened. "Well, I think we're off to a great start." Art was the language of her heart, and learning a new medium was challenging and thrilling.

Tessa rolled her eyes and leaned over the table. "She's totally modest about it, but she's a famous artist."

"I'm not famous," Claire quickly corrected. "No. I'm really not."

Tessa hooked a thumb at her friend. "She's the one who paints all those landscapes in the Art and Soul Gallery on Oak Street."

Heath's eyes widened. "You're C. Odom?"

Claire felt the heat tingle in her cheeks and a familiar pricking behind her eyes. She hated living in a constant state of embarrassment. She'd been shy most of her life, but the last few years had bumped things up a notch. Her body's central nervous system was constantly at work, making her uncomfortable to go along with her usual shy demeanor.

"She's *the* C. Odom! I don't know why she's even in my art class. She could make a masterpiece with toothpaste." Tessa waved her hand in the air, indicating the whimsy of Claire's talent.

"It's not like that." Claire rubbed a hand over her hair and down her ponytail. She liked being the anonymous hand behind the paintings. All she really did was create renderings. It was simple—visualize the scene and use the paint to recreate the image.

"Oh, it *is* like that," Tessa said. "What you do isn't normal."

Claire's chest ached. It wasn't that she desired to be normal, but it was never fun being reminded just how different she was from everyone else.

"Hey." Tessa's gentle hand reached for Claire's. "That's a good thing. You're exceptional."

"I agree," Heath said. "Those paintings are popular. Mom loves them."

Claire raised her head at Heath's words. It was silly to think he meant it. He was just agreeing with his sister.

"Have you been in the gallery lately?" Tessa asked. "She has a new series on Freedom Falls that is lit."

Heath squinted at his sister. "Are kids saying lit again?"

Tessa rolled her eyes. "Yes, you're so old that your vintage slang is coming back into style. We'll be wearing bell-bottoms before you know it."

Claire bit her lips between her teeth to contain her laughter. The sibling back-and-forth was easing the tension in her jaw and shoulders.

Heath shook his head at Tessa. "Bell-bottoms were before my time, and I hope they never make a comeback."

"Not here, anyway. Can you imagine dragging the soggy bottoms of your jeans through this snow?" Tessa asked, looking at Claire as if waiting for a response.

"No. I never really kept up with the latest styles anyway."

Their waitress brought their drinks, and Tessa took a long drink of her root beer. "You don't need trends. Who cares what you wear? You're a natural beauty."

Claire felt the pricking of sweat beading on the back of her neck. Any mention of her looks made her hands clammy. "Um, thanks."

Tessa squinted and mouthed, "Sorry." She knew why Claire had such an odd reaction to the subject, but the regret in her friend's expression said she'd forgotten.

Claire nodded once, acknowledging her friend's apology. It should have been nothing, but Tessa knew it was something.

Heath's gaze was toggling back and forth, trying to discern what he'd missed. "So, what is this about an art display at the ceremony tomorrow?"

Tessa sat up straighter. "Claire and I have new stained glass pieces we'll be sharing. Mine is a lantern, and hers is a… Well, it's something else."

Heath narrowed his eyes, questioning. "That's pretty vague."

"I can't tell you. It's a surprise," Tessa said.

Heath looked to Claire. Her skin grew warm at his friendly smile. "I guess I'll have to find out for myself tomorrow night."

Tessa tapped on her phone as the pizza arrived. She showed Heath a series of photos of the lantern she'd been working on for weeks while they devoured the hot dinner.

It had been ages since Claire had eaten in a restaurant. It was easier to order in or eat with her parents at their house.

Who was she kidding? Of course it was easier for a coward to order in. She'd made a life of staying out of public areas as much as possible. At least the ones that were crowded. She still went hiking with her dad every week on his day off. It was the only time they had to spend together, and Claire wasn't brave enough to venture out on her own to look for the landmarks and hidden places she replicated in her paintings.

"Wow. That's awesome, Tess," Heath said after finishing up his second slice.

Tessa dramatically flipped her hair over a shoulder. "I know. I'm considering changing my major to fine art."

Heath huffed. "Again? How many majors is that now?"

"Five!" Tessa shouted. "I'm allowed to change my mind," she defended.

"That you are. I just hope you find the one you're really looking for. Preferably before I kick the bucket."

Tessa tapped a greasy finger against her cheek, leaving an orange smudge. "You're a thirty-year-old bodyguard, and extreme winter sports are your thrill of choice. I say I may have ten years to make up my mind."

Heath wiped his hands on a rumpled napkin. "You'll be stuck with me longer than that if I have any say in it."

Claire listened as the siblings bantered. Their casual rapport was something she'd always wished she'd have with a sibling or cousin. Unfortunately, she'd been an only child, and her relatives lived on the east coast.

She'd had one true friend in college—her room-mate—and that relationship had fallen apart piece by piece after Claire's attack. It had been difficult to keep in touch after she moved back to Freedom. Eventually, they'd stopped calling each other. Claire had changed, and she'd never blamed her friend for their falling-out.

"I just don't know what I want to do with my life. This is a big decision," Tessa said, pulling Claire out of her thoughts.

"It is, but I know you can do anything you set your mind to. You're a Mitchell," Heath reminded his sister.

"I know." Tessa rested her chin in her hand and her shoulders slumped. "I'll never be able to measure up to Cora and Rachel, though."

"This isn't about them. You don't want to be an accountant, do you?" he asked.

"No way," Tessa said with a sour face.

"Army?"

Tessa shook her head. "Definitely not."

"Then it sounds like you're not our sisters, and you don't have to be measured against them. They're good at what they do, but you have to find *your* thing."

Tessa picked at her pizza. "Maybe I could—"

"Nope. You can't work for me," Heath said resolutely.

"Oh, come on!" Tessa whined. "I need better experience for my resume."

"Sorry. There's too much at stake in my line of work."

Tessa folded her arms. "Are you saying I'm incapable?"

"No. I'm saying the risk of *you* getting hurt is too high, and you're my little sister. That's all."

Claire over-chewed another bite of her pizza as she listened to the exchange. Was Tessa serious about working for Heath? Being a bodyguard sounded dangerous. People didn't hire security unless they knew the added protection might be necessary.

"I just want to do something important," Tessa said.

Heath pushed his plate to the side and leaned his arms on the table. "And you will, but you have to find your own path."

With a huff, Tessa leaned back. "Fine. I'll keep wandering around in my college career. I may just keep taking classes until they decide I'm qualified to teach something one day."

"I loved college," Claire said. It was a small enough addition to the conversation, but the ease that the words slipped out surprised her.

"Yeah, you went to SCAD. Of course you loved it."

"What's SCAD?" Heath asked.

"Savannah College of Art and Design," Tessa said. "I'm telling you, Claire is a legit artist."

"I've never heard of it, but it sounds impressive." Heath picked up the ticket that sat on the edge of the table and scooted out of the booth. "I'll be right back."

Claire fumbled for her purse. "Is he paying the bill?"

"Yeah. He's got it. Don't worry. He always buys my dinner."

"Your dinner," Claire said. "He doesn't have to buy mine." Claire nudged Tessa. "Let me out so I can pay him for my part."

"Don't be silly. Heath's got it. He wouldn't have taken the bill if he wasn't okay with paying it. He's not a beat-around-the-bush kind of guy."

Claire craned her neck to see Heath standing at the checkout counter. He wore a long-sleeve gray thermal shirt tucked into black cargo pants. Heavy black boots topped off his dark and dangerous look, but he had a casual, friendly demeanor that balanced out the intimidation she might have felt at his size. Not to mention he was handsome in a very obvious way. It had been years since Claire had looked at a man with interest, and it seemed oddly unfair that her best friend's brother was the one to spark that long-dampened desire.

"He's also single," Tessa whispered.

"Tessa!" Claire whispered a little too loudly. "I'm not—"

"I know you're not looking, but when *will* you be looking?"

Claire turned her attention away from her friend. "I don't know. Maybe that's not what my life is supposed to be like."

"You can lock yourself away in your studio and

create beautiful art for the rest of your life if that will make you happy. If you know in your heart that you won't be satisfied living a life without love, then I think that might be God telling you it's time to get out of your comfort zone."

Claire scoffed. "*Everything* is out of my comfort zone."

Tessa rested a hand on Claire's shoulder. "And with good reason. I know why you haven't pursued a relationship before, but maybe it's time to think about at least giving it a shot." Tessa tilted her head to where Heath lifted his hand in farewell to the cashier. "Heath would never hurt you. Maybe he could help you get used to dating again."

Claire frowned. "I don't want to use him like that."

"I'm not saying use him. I'm saying really go for it if you're interested in him."

Heath returned to the table and picked up his coat. "Isn't it past your bedtime, Tess? It's a school night."

"Ha-ha. You got me there, *Heathen*." She emphasized the last word as if the joke were a familiar one between them.

Heath waved, coaxing them out of the booth. "Come on. I have some more work to do."

"Do you sleep?" Tessa asked.

Claire rested the strap of her purse on her

shoulder and grinned, knowing she intended to put in a few more hours of work before bed, too.

"Not when there's work to do," Heath answered.

Tessa picked up the box containing her leftover pizza and gasped. "I forgot! I have to feed and walk the Hendersons' dog!"

Heath looked at his watch. "Way to go. Don't change your major to dog sitting."

Tessa frowned. "I have to run. Claire, is it okay if Heath walks you to your car?"

She'd parked in the lot on Spruce Street two blocks away. When she looked to Heath to gauge his reaction, he didn't seem put out by the offer his sister had made without asking him.

"Um, I don't want to be a bother. I can make it by myself." Even as she said the words, she could feel a panic attack rising in her throat.

Heath gestured for Tessa and Claire to lead the way out of the restaurant. "I insist. I've been sitting at my desk all week and need to stretch my legs."

Heath and Claire waved to Tessa as she crossed the street at the first intersection, leaving the two of them alone for the first time.

Christmas lights and garland adorned most everything on the Freedom Main Square, and instead of finding comfort in the signs of the coming Christmas season, the milling of people was a constant distraction that sent her anxiety into overdrive. How could she possibly watch everything around her? How could she anticipate danger when her head jerked right and left constantly?

"Are you okay?" Heath asked.

Claire's gaze darted around—to the stage, to the decorated gazebo in the square, to the laughing group of women stepping out of Giovanni's.

"I'm fine."

Having Heath beside her slightly eased her panic. It also helped that the snow-covered streets of Freedom were nothing like the hot and humid Savannah squares.

She pulled a hand from her coat pocket to point at her inconspicuous gray Jeep Grand Cherokee. "That's my car."

Heath looked over his shoulder, checking the street as they prepared to cross, but his attention caught on something behind them. In an instant, his expression changed to hard lines.

Claire's heart jumped into her throat, and she whirled around. A dark car was speeding down the road toward them.

The car and time seemed to slow as Claire watched its course changed slightly until the head-lights were pointed directly at Heath and herself. There wasn't anything distinct about the car, but Claire's breath caught in her lungs as Heath spun to her and wrapped his arms around her.

Then, she was falling fast. Her small frame gave way to the force of Heath's tackle, and they were both rushing toward the ground.

Her body hit hard with a jar that had her lungs screaming and her teeth snapping hard against each other. The roaring of the car's engine was deafening as the vehicle careened onto the sidewalk where they'd been standing less than two seconds ago.

Heath's body lay over hers, and the sudden weight left her unsure if the car had missed them or not. She couldn't see around him or breathe, for that matter.

There were bumps and a crash of metal before the roaring seemed to quiet. Claire gasped for breath and panic seized her when she couldn't suck in the air she needed.

Heath planted his hands in the snow on both sides of her and looked over his shoulder in the direction the vehicle had gone. Then his attention jerked back to her. Fear darkened his brown eyes, and the muscles in his neck were taut with tension.

Instead of trying and failing to suck air into her lungs, she exhaled, and a small breath pushed past her cold lips.

"Are you okay? Claire, say something," he begged.

When her lungs recovered, her first breath was a blood-curdling scream.

3

HEATH

*C*laire's scream pierced his ears as she flailed and scrambled away. Her eyes were closed tight, and her teeth were gritted in fear.

Heath rose to his feet and put his hands in the air. "Claire, it's me. I won't hurt you."

Tears streaked from the edges of her eyes and into her hair. She panted hard, sucking in deep lungfuls of the freezing air.

Heath kept his hands up as he turned to survey their surroundings. The car that had jumped the curb, left a tire track in the snow, and leveled a nearby mailbox was nowhere in sight.

"Claire, are you okay? Don't move. Just tell me if anything hurts."

She gasped for breath, and the look of terror was still painted on her face.

The door of the nearest house opened, and the porch light flicked on. A woman stepped out wearing a fuzzy pink robe that she tucked tighter around her body. "What was that?"

Heath lifted a hand to wave. "A vehicle came onto the sidewalk where we were walking."

The woman's hand covered her mouth for a moment. "Should I call for help?"

Heath looked back to Claire, who shivered. He lifted his head to the woman. "Yes, please."

The lady disappeared back into her house, and Heath continued to study Claire for obvious injuries. He squatted next to her. "Claire, are you okay? Please let me check you for injuries."

The impact of what had just happened hadn't settled in yet. He couldn't be sure, but Heath had a strong feeling the driver of that car had intended to hit them.

Claire sat shaking and panting in the snow. The sight of her fear gutted him. She'd been terrified all night, and now this.

With her chin tucked close to her chest, she bit her lips between her teeth and shook her head. "I'm sorry."

Sorry? None of this was her fault.

"Did you recognize that car?" he asked.

"No. I'm sorry I screamed at you. I thought… I was scared."

31

Heath rested his arms on his knees and linked his fingers. He hated this—hated seeing Claire so upset and scared. "I'm fine. It's you I'm worried about."

Her shoulder shook with her sobs. "I panicked."

"Do you think you can get up?" She had to be freezing from sitting in the snow. The cold wetness had settled through his own pants since they'd fallen.

Claire nodded and wiped her face.

Heath wound his arms under hers and helped her stand. Her shaking intensified, and he grappled with the urge to hold her. Would she want that? Tears still streaked down her cheeks. Did she need a literal shoulder to cry on?

The homeowner stepped outside again. "Help is on the way."

Claire lifted her head. "I'm fine. I don't need a paramedic or anything." She shook her head. "This is just…embarrassing."

"I'd still feel better if someone took a look. Plus, we'll need to file a report about this."

Heath released her to remove his coat and gently draped it over Claire's shoulders. She had to be freezing from sitting in the snow, but it was the best comfort he could give. He had the distinct feeling that touching her would incite the panic again.

"Thank you," she whispered.

She continued to shake, and Heath wasn't sure if it was from the cold or shock.

"Claire, I know you're scared, but I need you to tell me if anything hurts. Are you injured?"

After a short pause, she shrugged, which caused her to wince. "My back hurts."

"From the fall? I'm really sorry about that. I didn't have much time to think."

"No, thank you. I wasn't thinking as quickly as you were."

Heath ran a hand through his hair. The adrenaline pumping through his system warmed his muscles, even after he'd given up his coat.

The woman shuffled toward them in her house robe. "Goodness, child. You're freezing. Please come inside."

Heath nodded, encouraging Claire to take the woman up on her offer.

The police arrived just as the women went inside, and Heath went to meet the officer on the street.

It was the new guy, Ty Riggs. Heath had run into him a few times in town, but this was their first meeting in the scope of business.

"Heath, should I say it's good to see you?" Ty said, holding his hand out.

Heath shook it. "I'm not sure yet."

"Tell me what's going on."

Heath looked at the tire tracks in the muddy snow. "I was walking my sister's friend to the parking lot on Spruce Street. A car was coming down this road, and when it got closer to us, it came up onto the sidewalk and almost hit us." Even recounting the incident sent a chill down his spine.

"Were there any witnesses?" Ty asked.

"Not that I know of. The woman who lives here came outside after it happened. I'm sure she heard it."

"Heard it?"

Heath pointed to the black mailbox attached to a wooden post that lay in the yard. "And Claire was screaming after."

He decided to leave out his opinion on the reason for her momentary panic. He had a feeling it had more to do with the reason she'd been looking over her shoulder all night than the vehicle that could have killed them both in two seconds flat. He looked at the crumpled mailbox and fought a shudder. They could have easily ended up under that car. "I think it scared her, but I'd like to get her checked out if you have a paramedic on the way."

"One is en route. Show me approximately where the vehicle left the road."

Heath walked with Ty the few steps to the place just before the tracks in the snow began. Ty took some photos and listened while Heath recounted the incident.

The paramedics arrived a minute later, and Claire stepped outside to speak with the man and woman. Heath gave her some space as they checked her vitals, and she gave her own report to them and Ty.

The kind woman who'd called for help and given Claire a cup of coffee and an extra blanket stood on the porch watching while the first responders crowded her small yard. The scene looked odd. Heath had always known Freedom as a fairly safe place, but tonight this part of the quiet town looked like a crime scene.

He hadn't decided if he thought it was an actual crime scene or not.

He stepped up beside the woman and leaned against the porch column. "Thank you for helping and welcoming Claire into your home."

"Oh, of course. The poor girl looked shell-shocked."

What did the woman know about shell-shock? It wasn't something he'd wish on his worst enemies.

"I appreciate your kindness. I'm Heath Mitchell."

She held out an aged hand, keeping the other tucked warmly around her. "Beverly Gray. You take good care of her." It was more of a gentle reminder than an acknowledgment.

"I will." He wasn't sure how just yet, but he intended to check in on Claire. Something about tonight coupled with her unease from earlier didn't sit right with him.

Ty met Heath and Ms. Gray on the porch. "I have a few more questions for you."

"Lay it on me," Heath said.

"Any chance you got a tag number?"

"I thought about it, but the vehicle was too far away by the time I could look up."

"That's understandable. Just needed to ask. You need to see the paramedics?" Ty pointed over his shoulder at the couple who were still talking to Claire.

"No, but thanks for everything." Heath rubbed a hand through his hair and warred with himself for a moment. "I have no factual basis for this statement, but I got the impression we were targeted."

Ty's brows rose. "Really?"

"Like I said, don't take it to the bank, but it's a straight road, and we were well off the shoulder. The vehicle seemed to drift toward us at the perfect time."

"I'll keep that in mind as I finish up my investigation."

Heath gave Ms. Gray his business card and thanked her again, making a mental note to hand-deliver some of Jan Clark's baked goods from Stories and Scones to her later in the week.

The paramedics were saying their farewells when Heath stepped into the yard where Claire had a blanket wrapped around her shoulders.

He took a deep breath of the biting winter air. The rush of fire in his veins needed to cool off. "You okay?"

Claire nodded.

"Can I take you to a doctor? There's an after-hours clinic in the next town."

"No, I'm okay."

Heath's hand dragged through his hair. "I'm really sorry about taking you down so hard."

"I'm glad you did. Otherwise, we might not be having this conversation right now."

Good. At least she understood how close they'd come to a fatal incident tonight.

"I'll walk you to your car."

"I left my purse inside. I'll be right back."

Despite her assurance, Heath didn't feel like letting her out of his sight. It was irrational, but he needed to see with his own eyes that she was okay.

They said another thankful good-bye to Ms. Gray and started again toward the parking lot on the next block.

Claire shivered. "We were so close."

Heath could see the lot where she'd pointed out her car earlier.

"Can I follow you home? I want to make sure you get there safely."

Claire shook her head. "No. Thanks, but I'm fine."

"I really don't mind. I'm worried about you."

She turned to him with a small smile. "I'm beginning to understand that. I'm okay from here."

She unlocked the door to her Jeep, and he opened it. She pulled her arms from his coat and offered it back to him.

He held up a hand. "No. You keep it. It'll be a minute before your car heats up. Do you live far from here?"

"Thanks. No, I'm not far."

He wanted to ask if she had someone to check on her, but he sensed that the questions made her uncomfortable.

As she slipped into her vehicle, loss and concern grew within him. "Good night. Drive safe."

"I will. Thanks for everything."

Heath backed up as she drove from the lot. What now? He was always the one with the plan. He knew the next step, but he felt lost as Claire drove away. Surely, the danger was over. What were the chances she'd end up in another life-threatening situation?

He pulled his cell from his pocket and called his sister as he walked back into the heart of downtown Freedom.

Tessa answered with too much pep for the late hour. "Hey. Working hard or hardly working?"

"I'm not working. Claire and I ran into trouble

on the way to her car. She just now started on her way home."

Tessa's tone changed to alarmed. "What do you mean? Heath, what happened to her?"

Heath puffed a breath of hot air that billowed in a cloud in front of his mouth. "Nothing, thankfully. A car came off the road and almost hit us on the sidewalk."

"Is she okay?"

"It didn't hit us," Heath hurried to explain.

"No, I mean, how was she?"

Heath thought he knew what his sister was asking, but he still wasn't sure about Claire's nervousness or the cause of it. "She was okay, I guess. She panicked a little when I tackled her."

"Good grief. I've gotta go."

"Wait. What is she so scared of?" Heath asked quickly.

"I don't think she'd appreciate it if I told you."

"Can I have her number? I'd like to check on her too and see if she needs anything."

Tessa hummed. "I don't think she'd want me to do that without asking first. I'll find out tonight and let you know."

He could understand that. He also knew he could be patient and respect her privacy. "Thanks. Just let me know."

"Thanks for saving her. I'm glad you were there."

"Are you going to check on her? She wouldn't let me follow her home, and I want to make sure she's okay. It was kind of traumatic."

"I'll check on her. Say a prayer for her, please."

"Of course." If he could do nothing else, he could pray. The Lord had certainly had His hand in the events of the evening.

"Love you."

"Love you too. Will you let me know how she is?"

"Yes. Gotta go."

Heath disconnected the call, fighting the urge to prod his sister with more questions about Claire.

He tried to reason that his curiosity was fueled by the mystery that surrounded her. In truth, it was a combination of lots of things—her meek demeanor, her kind disposition, her constant worry, and her natural beauty that he'd tried to ignore all evening.

For now, all he could do was wait and hope his sister knew how to be there for Claire.

4

CLAIRE

The smell of fresh coffee and sweet cinnamon rolls greeted Claire the next morning, but another scent mingled in her senses. Pine and spice mixed with frost brought her right back to the events of last night.

Heath. She'd worn his coat home, and she'd clung to it through the night.

It was a little pathetic, but there wasn't anyone here to judge her. The smell had calmed her and reminded her of his strength and comfort.

Going back to her quiet, empty house after everything that happened last night hadn't seemed like a good idea. Instead, she'd driven straight to her parents' house.

She pushed out of bed and stretched her arms over her head. Her back and neck were a little sore.

She'd hit the ground hard when Heath had pushed her out of the way of the wayward vehicle.

Claire picked up her glasses from the nightstand and made her way into the kitchen. She hated wearing her glasses, especially while working, but her stomach's inclination for the fresh breakfast was more intense than her desire to see clearly.

Her mom stood at the sink washing blueberries.

"Morning," Claire said as she pulled a mug from the cabinet.

"Morning, sweetie. How did you sleep?"

"Restlessly." She'd expected the nightmares, but last night had been mingled with new memories of a dark vehicle speeding toward her while her feet were stuck in a block of cement.

"You can take a nap this afternoon," her mom said as she moved the blueberries to a decorative bowl.

"Actually, I need to eat and run. I have work to do."

"Honey, you can slow down for one day."

Claire spent a lot of time in her studio, but painting was more than a job. The passion she'd pursued in her young life had become the therapy she'd needed after the incident that had stolen the last of her college career. Now, her drive to create paid the bills, which was one less thing she had to worry about.

"I'm almost finished with this week's series."

"Oh, I forgot to tell you. Your dad isn't coming home this week."

Claire's shoulders sank. "Really? Why?"

Her dad was a truck driver, but he came home two days a week. He usually spent one of those days hiking in the Freedom area with Claire.

"He broke down in Boise and needs to make up the hours."

She knew it was silly, but Claire lived a scheduled life. There were fewer surprises and unexpected messes if everything stayed the same. Unfortunately, life didn't always fall into her plan.

Claire was silent as she watched the coffee dripping into the carafe.

Her mom's hand rested on her shoulder. "I know how much you enjoy that time with him, but maybe we could go shopping instead."

It wasn't just that she enjoyed the peaceful time with her dad. Those treks into the wilderness fueled the creativity she put into her paintings that week. Each adventure produced six paintings that she sold to the Art and Soul Gallery in town.

She'd never been a starving artist, only because she'd figured out a way to beat the system. Her paintings were sold before they were even created.

She thought of those trips with her dad as the filling of her cup. When the cup was empty, the paintings stopped. She'd painted herself into a self-induced creative block.

"Thanks for the offer. I'll let you know."

"I think you should stay here for a while," her mom said solemnly. "You almost died last night."

"Mom, I don't think…" Claire began to argue, but she truly had almost died last night. She hadn't been able to wrap her head around the implications of what had happened yet.

"I just worry about you," her mom said as she set her own cup beside the coffeemaker.

Claire chuckled. "I thought worrying was my job. Trust me, I do enough of that for the both of us."

Her mom brushed a hand over Claire's hair. "You've been through so much. I can't bear the thought of something else happening to you."

"I'm okay, Mom." At least that's what she was telling herself. She was still standing, and that was better than the alternative. She hugged her mom and breathed in the comfort of home.

"You should stay here. You know we like it better when you're here."

Claire appreciated her mom's concern. She'd been blessed with parents who would do anything for her and loved her immensely. But after hearing Heath encourage his sister last night, she wondered if her parents' extreme concern was enabling her predisposition to sit safely on the sidelines. Her parents hadn't encouraged her to do anything outside of the comfortable box she lived in since that night she was attacked in Georgia.

"How is Women's Wonders?" Claire asked, knowing once her mom started in about the philanthropy group at church, she'd be safely away from any talk about staying here.

Claire was thankful to have parents who cared, but she was often ashamed of her dependence on them. She was almost thirty, and she hardly ventured more than ten miles from her own home or her parents'. Shouldn't she be making her own way and climbing the success ladder? She knew lots of other women her age were flourishing in their careers.

And she did consider herself successful, but it wasn't in the showy, go-get-'em way that society glamorized. She wasn't a businesswoman in a suit crushing gender norms, but she loved her peaceful life.

After breakfast, Claire helped her mom clean up the kitchen and said good-bye. Her mom insisted Claire stay for the day, but the more she thought about it, the more she knew leaving was the right choice.

Her inclination had always been to stay, but after witnessing Heath and Tessa's strong wills the night before, Claire knew she wanted some of that bravery.

When she pulled into the short drive leading to her house three minutes later, the distance from her mom seemed much greater than the reality. Had she made the right decision to come home?

She parked her Jeep and grabbed her purse and Heath's coat just as her phone began ringing. The incident from the night before still had her on high alert, so she ignored the phone call in favor of keeping her attention focused on the yard, street, and nearby houses.

Inside, she breathed in the warmer air and hung her keys, coat, and scarf on the rack beside the door. She surveyed every visible surface, but her home was exactly as she'd left it.

She was generally self-aware of her tendency to overreact, but the near hit-and-run from the night before wasn't anything to gloss over. It wasn't every day she found herself in the path of a speeding vehicle.

Then again, she'd come to realize that she wasn't exempt from the dangers of life, and despite her hatred of the feeling, she lived every day in fear of the next unexpected tragedy.

Claire pulled her phone from her purse before hanging it on the rack and saw Tessa's missed call.

They'd talked for a few minutes last night, but Claire had been too busy trying to calm her mom's panic.

It was laughable. What a pair Claire and her mom made. Two worrywarts fussing over something that had already happened was like the blind leading the blind.

Claire made her way into the studio at the back of her house. It had once been a spare bedroom, but now it housed the mess that created the art. The chemical smell of oil-based paint and turpentine welcomed her to work.

Her first order of business was to open the windows and door leading to the backyard. The guest room had been perfect for the studio because she needed ample light and ventilation.

When the windows were opened and the cool air of the Rockies drifted into the studio, Claire returned Tessa's call.

"Hey, how are you?" Tessa answered.

Claire switched the call to speakerphone and left it on the wooden desk as she grabbed a paint-stained apron. "I'm okay. I just got home from Mom and Dad's."

"You want me to come keep you company? I don't have any classes today."

"No, I'm fine." Claire pulled her hair up into a bun and sighed.

"You don't sound fine. It's my job as your friend to call you out on it if you're lying."

"I'm not lying. Really, I'm fine. I'm just bummed that my dad isn't coming home this week."

Claire looked at the easels lined up on the long, custom table her dad had built for her. The series from last week only needed a few finishing touches. She picked up her stool and plopped it down in front of the painting that needed the most work.

"What a bummer. I know how much you enjoy that time with him. Will you be able to push through with new paintings next week?"

Claire grabbed her pallet and smiled. Tessa was Claire's complete opposite, but she appreciated her friend's concern. Others would have scoffed and thought it was silly that she hit a creative roadblock when her father-daughter hikes were interrupted, but Tessa understood Claire's quirks.

"I can, but I probably won't be able to offer those to the gallery. They're never my best work when the memory isn't fresh."

"I'm amazed at your process. I have no idea how you can see something in the woods and make a painting that looks just like it. I wish I could do that."

"There are a lot of things you do that I wish I could do," Claire said as she dipped a fan brush in a cool-white and ultramarine-blue mixture.

48

Tessa scoffed. "Like what? Get kicked out of chemistry?"

"I can't believe you did that," Claire said with a smile.

"How was I supposed to know mixing bleach and vinegar was dangerous?"

"You're the only one who doesn't know that."

"Whatever. I wasn't planning to be a chemist anyway."

Claire stroked the paint over the layer from yesterday, mixing in the radiant magenta that warmed the sky. "I wish I could make friends as easily as you do," Claire whispered.

Tessa sighed. "I know why it's hard for you to put yourself out there." Her tone perked. "But you might want to look into making more friends like Heath."

Claire's face heated at the mention of Heath. The more she'd thought about her fear from last night, the more images of Heath pried their way into her mind. It *would* be nice to have a friend like Heath—strong, kind, and brave.

"I'm glad he was there," Claire said. "I can't explain how quickly he moved when he saw the car coming toward us. I just stood there like a statue, but it was as if his instinct was to…"

Claire let the sentence hang, uncomfortable with the assessment she'd almost made.

"To save you? Oh, because that *is* his instinct. He's

a highly trained bodyguard. He's worked in security since I was in middle school. He knows what he's doing."

Tessa's assessment of her brother was admirable, and now Claire knew it to be the truth. She could see why his reaction was spot-on due to his career that revolved around quick decision-making skills. She felt the same adeptness when she picked up a paintbrush.

"I get what you're saying, but I doubt I'll be calling up Heath to hang out anytime soon."

Tessa hummed. "Well, there is the Tree Lighting Ceremony tonight."

Claire twisted her neck to both sides, stretching the tense muscles. "I don't think I'm going."

"But your statue is in the art display."

Claire sighed, warring with her instinct to revert further into her shell after last night's incident. "I just don't feel comfortable going back there again." They'd been barely two blocks away from the main downtown square when the car had almost hit them.

"I get it, but Heath already said he'd come. He could be there with us, and you wouldn't have anything to worry about."

Claire studied the pallet in her hand. It was coated with the bright whites and earthy colors of the Freedom landscapes. The hues were light and hopeful to match Tessa's personality, but Claire's soul felt dreary like a stormy night.

"I don't think I can," Claire repeated.

"That's okay. I'll get your statue after the display is over."

"You don't have to do that. I'll come get it."

"Nah. It'll be a piece of cake. Mine is small, and I'll have Heath to help me with yours. We'll run it by your place before we head home."

Claire recalled Heath's offer to follow her home the night before. At the time, she thought she'd been guarding her peaceful, secluded life. Now that she'd had half a day to process Heath's genuine kindness, she didn't see the problem in him knowing where she lived. It seemed silly to think Heath would ever seek to do her harm.

"Thanks. I'd planned to go, but after—"

"I know," Tessa interrupted. "Last night was a step back for you. I know you're capable of taking back your life, but you have to come to that conclusion on your own before anything is going to change."

Claire gently stroked the fan brush through the paint mixture. She couldn't wait for the day she told her fears to take a hike. She just didn't feel strong enough to do it today. "I'm working on it."

"Have you thought about setting up a security system for your home? Or getting an emergency alert app on your phone? I'm sure Heath could do any of those things. If you felt safer, maybe you could venture out more."

It wasn't a bad idea. She had a basic home security system, but she'd never really been worried that someone might seek her out at home. The man who'd attacked her could be anywhere in the world right now, and he hadn't tried to come after her. He'd been out of prison for two years, and she hadn't heard a peep about him.

"I have a home security system, but I like your idea about the emergency alert. Maybe I would feel better if I knew I could call for help quickly."

"I'll send you Heath's number. You don't have to use it, although it is advised," Tessa said with a smile in her voice.

"Thanks. I'll think about it."

"And I'll be praying," Tessa said.

"Thanks."

Claire had prayed endlessly in the first months after the attack. Most of those pleas had been born of her fear. Later, they turned angry and hollow.

Years later, she'd begun to pray again with a more mature outlook on prayer. She'd been selfishly shouting at God to take away the pain of the past, but now she wondered if she should have been praying for peace and strength all along. She was ashamed of those incoherent ramblings directed at the God who loved her. It had taken longer than she cared to admit to realize that the attack wasn't God's fault.

There had been times, even through the praying, when she'd felt hopeless and distant from God. Now, she prayed for forgiveness for those times when her faith had faltered.

"Love you!" Tessa said cheerily.

"Love you too."

Claire pressed the button to disconnect the call and felt the weight of the silence settle around her. She clipped her brush in a holder and used her pinky finger—the one that was free of paint—to pull up her painting playlists. She had groups of music she chose based on her mood and the scenes she painted.

Today, she was in an instrumental mood. The soft sounds were a contrast to her turbulent heart.

She picked up her brush as the first notes of the symphony began, but she knew there was no hope for inspiration today. Her heart wasn't in the scenes lined before her.

With a defeated sigh, she left her pallet and brush to gather the materials she needed to make canvases for next week's set.

She loved the building stage as much as the final product. The force of the drill pushed against her as she made holes in each piece of wood and fastened them together with screws. She stretched the canvas and secured it around the boards with the staple gun. She showered and cleaned up the house while the gesso dried. Her mom had called twice by the time she started the sanding and second coat of primer.

When she'd stalled enough, she looked at the unfinished set. Was she putting off finishing them because she didn't know what to do next?

The longer she delayed, the more difficult it would be to put the final touches on them. Still, her attention drifted to a set of canvases in a corner—the ones she'd marred while making and couldn't use for pieces she intended to sell.

She picked up a fresh canvas and pulled the plastic wrap off another pallet. The one covered in deep blues and vivid purples was set aside for therapy painting.

Hours later, the canvas was a swirling mix of midnight blue and vivid red—the colors of the sky the night she'd thought death had come for her.

5

HEATH

*H*eath parked in front of his parents' house. The dash clock read 4:12, but he'd be waiting on Tessa for the next half hour. She was notoriously late, but this time, he'd told her to be ready earlier, and he'd taken his time picking her up.

Inside his parents' house, everything was the same as it had been his whole life. Family photos hung on the wall, the garland was already hanging across the mantle above the fireplace, and the smell of his mom's favorite gardenia candle filled the room.

"Just a second!" Tessa screamed from the second floor.

Heath huffed. She'd need more than a second, so he settled in on the couch to check his emails and messages. Got Your Six had gotten the bid on a security job for an art auction in Texas in January, so he forwarded the details to Adam.

Within seconds, Adam's name lit up the cell phone screen.

"Hey."

"Hey, boss. You in on this one?" Adam asked, eager to get to work and handle business.

"I think that's the best option. The two of us should be enough to cover it. Jeremiah can run things that weekend."

"I'll book our flights now," Adam said, always thinking five steps into the future.

"It'll keep till tomorrow. You not going to the Tree Lighting Ceremony tonight?"

"Nah, my grandparents are in town, but they don't get around well. I'll probably hang around here with them. Kick some tail at Rummy or Old Maid."

Heath imagined his stern, burly friend entertaining his grandparents. "I can't say the Tree Lighting Ceremony is the most entertaining event I've ever attended, but it might be better than card games."

"You going solo?" Adam asked.

"Just Tessa. She's taking her sweet, precious time."

"Some things never change."

Heath had asked Adam to pick Tessa up at the

airport once, and the two had clashed over Tessa's dawdling. Apparently, Tessa had gone nose-to-nose with the ever-responsible Adam when he'd reprimanded her for being late.

Now, every time Tessa's name came up, Adam barely concealed his disdain for Heath's spunky sister. They were complete opposites, and he steered his friend and his sister in different directions whenever they ended up at the same gathering together.

"Yep. Slow as Christmas as usual."

Adam laughed. "No one in Freedom ever had to wait long for Christmas to come around."

"The square was ready to be lit last night." Heath sat up straighter. "Oh man, I didn't tell you what happened."

"At dinner with Tessa?"

"After we ate, I offered to walk Tessa's friend, Claire, to the lot on Spruce where she'd parked. A car came up onto the sidewalk and almost hit us."

"No way. That's wild."

"Tell me about it. We barely got out of the way in time."

"Was the driver drunk or something?"

"I don't know. He didn't stop."

"You get a tag number? Is Tessa's friend okay?"

"No tag number, but Claire is fine, I think. Tessa was supposed to check on her today. Claire mentioned last night that she was coming to the

Tree Lighting tonight, so I may be able to get an update in a little bit. She was shaken up for sure."

"I don't blame her. It's not every day you almost get hit by a car."

Adam's validation of the unlikeliness of the almost hit-and-run raised the hair on the back of Heath's neck. That feeling that it hadn't been accidental had stayed in the forefront of his mind since last night.

"I don't know anything about her, but she seemed nervous, even before the incident. It made me wonder if she's caught up in something dangerous."

"It can't be anything good if someone intended to hit her with a car. That's vehicular assault at the least."

Heath rubbed the stubble on his chin. "She doesn't seem like the criminal type."

"Maybe she needs our services. We could set up a remote surveillance system." Adam talked about intel gadgets the way some guys talked about sports.

"I'll ask Tessa if she thinks Claire might need that. I don't want to overstep. To say she was guarded last night was an understatement. That might be an invasion of her privacy."

"There are different degrees of surveillance. We could do something basic, like a remote exterior package."

"That might be okay."

"With window sensors," Adam added.

"Um…"

"And a perimeter alarm."

"We don't want her panicking every time a bunny hops onto her property," Heath said.

"Right. Okay. Scale it back," Adam said to himself.

"Maybe nix it altogether. She knows I'm in the security business, and she didn't ask for my help."

"It seems like a waste of our skills," Adam said.

Heath huffed. "Security isn't foolproof."

He'd built his career around recon. His talent was relying on intelligent communication systems. He'd invested his education in a system he'd once believed in.

But he'd been wrong once, and that was one time too many.

When Adam spoke again, his usual serious tone was deeper. It was what Heath had come to recognize as the pity voice. Everyone who knew about his big mistake used it at some point.

"One slip up doesn't mean we stop trying our best," Adam said.

Adam knew about Heath's past and the reason he'd left the Marines. It wasn't a slipup, it was a massive, fatal mistake. Two of his Marine brothers were dead, and he couldn't forgive himself.

"I know," Heath said. "That's why I'm still here." That and his sisters hadn't let him lie down and give up after he'd come home a broken shell of the man he'd once been.

Tessa's footsteps knocked on the stairs behind him. "I need to let you go. Count me in for January."

"You got it, Boss," Adam said as they disconnected the call.

Heath pushed the memories away and stood. "'Bout time."

"Oh, hush," Tessa said as she tied a scarf around her neck. "We'll be outside all night. I needed plenty of layers."

"Mission accomplished. You look like a stuffed teddy bear."

Tessa halted in the foyer and turned. "I need to change."

Heath grabbed her arm and spun her around. "No way. If you're riding with me, the train is leaving the station. We're already going to be parking ten blocks from the square."

Tessa contemplated for a moment before sighing. "Ugh. Fine."

Heath opened the car door for his sister, and she giggled.

"Guys don't open doors for women anymore."

Heath frowned. "They do. Don't lower your expectations because the kids you date are jokes."

Heath walked around the front of the car and

settled into the driver's seat. Tessa was oddly quiet. "What?" he asked.

"Nothing. Just thinking. I don't think I need a man to open my door." There was no bite in her statement. Her tone was more uncertain.

"It takes zero effort for you to open the door for yourself. Of course you don't need it. Does he need you to send him a good morning text? No, but it's nice, and why wouldn't you if you cared?"

All of Heath's sisters were fierce and independent. They could take care of themselves, and he treated them accordingly. But he'd always had a feeling Tessa's boldness was forced, as if she compared herself to Cora and Rachel.

"True. I guess Mama raised you right."

Heath merged onto the road headed toward downtown Freedom. "That doesn't explain why I'm still single."

He'd made the joke light-heartedly, but the words rang with truth that stung a little.

"You're single because you work too much."

"I don't work too much," Heath defended.

"It's not that you work too much. It's that you don't do anything else. When you're not at work, you're hanging out with your friends who are dudes, and they're married. If you're not with them, you're with me or Mom and Dad."

Heath watched the road ahead and rubbed a hand over the scruff on his cheek. "You got me there."

"Your only other opportunity to run into a single woman is at church," Tessa said.

"Nah. I took Heather Green on a date once, but we both knew that wasn't going to work out. She's nice, but we don't have anything in common."

Tessa laughed. "You mean you don't like cats?"

Heather was a nice girl, but she lived with no fewer than a dozen cats and wasn't interested in much else.

Heath shivered as a chill ran up his spine. "Not nearly as much as Heather."

They entered the downtown area, and Tessa sat forward in her seat. "Whoa. This place is packed!"

Cars were parked in the lots of every closed business on the outskirts of the downtown business district and along every sidewalk. Heath slowed and scanned the area for a place to park. "I told you we should have gotten here earlier."

Heath had attended the Tree Lighting Ceremony every year he'd been in town. It was a hit for locals and tourists alike, and he'd missed it a little when he'd been away with the Marines. Everyone in town came to the tree lighting, so it was always a good opportunity to catch up with people he might not have seen in a while.

This year, he'd agreed to go with Tessa, since

their parents were out of town visiting their aunt and uncle. Tessa was proud of the stained glass lantern she kept talking about, and Heath was her only family in town. He wanted to be that support for her.

They found a spot behind the local thrift store and grabbed coats, scarves, and gloves before starting their trek toward the square. The sidewalks leading into the heart of the town were full of people who merged into the road once they entered the area where the streets were blocked off for the event.

"I wish Claire could have come," Tessa said as they walked.

Heath's attention sharpened at the mention of Claire. "Why didn't she?"

"She was going to, but I think last night set her back a little."

"Set her back?"

"She doesn't like being out after dark. It's just a thing."

Tessa was clearly glossing over the true explanation, which only piqued Heath's interest.

"I thought she had something in the art display tonight."

"She does. I told her we'd bring it by her place after the tree lighting was over." Tessa grabbed Heath's arm, tugging him toward the stage.

"Speaking of the art display, let's go there first. I can't wait to show you what I made."

The display was set up in the grassy area near the church. Ground lights shone on the artwork, and bulb lights were hung from thin iron poles around the pieces. There were paintings, pottery, metal statues, and other things Heath didn't recognize.

Tessa tugged him to the far side where a rectangular, metal lantern hung from one of the poles supporting the string lights. "This one's mine."

Each side had a stained glass window surrounded by a small strip of metal. Tessa turned it slowly, showcasing the different windows—a snowman, a Christmas tree, a cross, and a dove.

"Whoa, Tess, that's awesome." Heath studied the windows, noting the frosted white of the snowman and the soft yellow of the light around the cross. "It's perfect."

"Not perfect, but pretty cool, right?"

"Definitely cool. Mom will want this one."

Tessa grinned. "I planned on giving it to her for Christmas."

Heath groaned. "What am I getting Mom for Christmas?" He'd never been good at understanding what women wanted as gifts. Having three sisters hadn't helped at all.

"She wants a spiralizer."

"I have no idea what that is," Heath admitted.

She patted his shoulder. "Don't worry about it. I'll order it."

"Thanks. You're a lifesaver."

"No, I just need your help getting Dad a gift."

Heath chuckled. "You got it." His dad was easy to buy for. Heath listened enough to know which tools his dad wanted, and there was an unspoken understanding that his dad expected to get them at Christmas.

Tessa grabbed his arm again. "Look at Claire's."

Heath turned to the tall, colorful statue, and his eyes widened. "That's what Claire made?"

Curves of colored glass wound up the three-dimensional, six-foot structure in flowing waves. It was wild and captivating. He couldn't put his finger on why, but he couldn't pry his attention away from it.

"Super cool, right?" Tessa prompted.

"For lack of a better way to describe it, yes, it's super cool. I get what you were saying about her artistic talent."

He stepped around the formation, studying the various colors and lighting. It didn't look like anything he'd seen before, and it was the first abstract piece of art he'd ever wanted to understand.

"I hate that she couldn't be here."

"Me too. It looks like she spent a lot of time on this. I hope it fits in my SUV."

Tessa gasped. "I didn't think about that. The teacher brought them all over in an enclosed trailer."

Heath slapped a hand on his sister's shoulder. "We can make it work."

Tessa lurched forward with the force of Heath's friendly pat. "Easy, *Heathen*. You don't know your own strength."

"Sorry. I forget you're delicate."

Tessa rolled her eyes. "Let's go get some hot chocolate. And I want peppermint bark."

"Aye, aye, Captain."

They stopped at Freedom Fudge Factory and got in the long line that ended on the sidewalk outside the bakery. Tessa danced on her toes and tucked her hands into her coat while Heath laughed at her theatrics.

When he looked up, Officer Ty Riggs was walking past wearing his uniform. Ty and Heath noticed each other at the same time.

"Hey, man," Heath said as he pulled a hand from his coat pocket.

"Hey. Good to see you in better circumstances," Ty said as they shook hands.

"This is my sister, Tessa. She's a good friend of Claire's."

Ty offered a hand to Tessa. "Officer Ty Riggs. How's Claire holding up today?"

"She's okay. Thanks so much for helping her out."

Ty tsked. "I'm not sure I did much. We had so little evidence to work with. It's unlikely we'll ever figure out who was driving that car."

"Oh, well. You did your best, and everyone is okay. I guess that's all that matters," Tessa said.

Ty nodded slowly. "I have to remember that myself sometimes. I have to head out. I'll catch up with you later."

Heath and Ty parted ways with slaps on the back.

After they each got a cup of hot chocolate from Stories and Scones, Tessa dragged Heath around the busy downtown square, stopping every few feet to chat with someone she knew. Heath knew most of them, but Tessa made a best friend out of everyone she met. By the time everyone began crowding around the stage for the tree lighting, they'd eaten donuts, peppermint bark, roasted chestnuts, and they'd each drunk a large cup of hot chocolate.

Tessa held up the last chocolate truffle. "It's yours if you want it."

Heath shook his head. "No way. I'm stuffed. I may have trouble waking up from this sugar coma in the morning."

Mayor Starling stepped up onto the stage and welcomed everyone to the annual Christmas Tree Lighting Ceremony. After a few announcements, he beckoned his wife to the stage where she told the age-old story of Freedom's beginning during the Gold Rush.

Heath scanned the crowd and noticed most everyone was paired up. A man draped his arm over a woman's shoulders, a mother hugged the child on her hip, and a young couple stood close with their heads resting together. The scene was idyllic and romantic. When would he be able to celebrate Christmas traditions with a woman beside him?

Tessa bounced on her toes, eager for the reveal. He should be content to be here with his sister. Some people didn't have family they could count on, and he was lucky to have at least that.

The countdown to the lighting began, but Heath couldn't find the motivation to participate. Thoughts of Claire zipped in and out of his head. Was she alone? Was she okay after last night? What did his sister know about Claire that she kept so heavily guarded?

Mayor Starling gave the signal, and the square lit with thousands of tiny lights. Whites, blues, greens, golds, and reds filled every inch of the crowded square, reflecting off the soft, white snow that settled on the canopies and trees.

Once the ceremony was complete, Tessa led the way back to Stories and Scones where she had Jan pack up some baked goods for Claire. Heath spotted his old friend, Pete, nearby and broke out of the line.

"Hey, how's business this year?" Heath asked.

Pete stood from the plush chair where he'd been sipping coffee and extended a hand to Heath. "Busy as usual."

"Busy is good, my friend," Heath said.

Pete rented out half a dozen cabins on the mountain, and his properties were always in high demand.

"I thank the Lord every day," Pete said, but his attention kept drifting to the bakery checkout counter.

Heath turned to see Jan and Tessa happily chatting as they decided on the best pastries for Claire. "Jan seems to be doing okay."

Pete cleared his throat. "I hope so. Aiden, Joanna, and James went to visit Joanna's parents for the weekend, so I've been walking her to her car after work."

Jan's son, Aiden, was one of Heath's good friends, and both Heath and Pete knew that Jan didn't need someone to walk her to her car after work. She was widowed, but she could take care of herself.

Heath rubbed a hand over his mouth to hide his grin. "That's nice of you. I bet she enjoys the company."

Pete shrugged. "I sure do."

Tessa waved good-bye to Jan and joined Heath and Pete where they stood by a bookshelf out of the way.

"Hey, Pete!" Tessa threw her arms around their family friend.

"Good to see you, Tess. How's school?"

"Great." Her brows drew closer together, and she tilted her head. "Hey, you looking for some help with your rentals or the insurance agency?" she asked.

Pete's brow rose. "Are you looking for a job?"

"Well, I was thinking it might be fun. Maybe I could be an insurance agent one day."

Pete chuckled. "Still haven't figured out what you want to be when you grow up?"

"It's such a big decision!" Tessa exclaimed.

"I can always use a hand," Pete said. "Stop by my office, and I'll put you on the payroll."

Heath wasn't sure what to think of Pete's offer, but he agreed that Tessa might need to get her toes in the water before she could figure out what she wanted to do.

Tessa smiled from ear to ear. "Thank you!" She held up the bag of goodies. "We have to head out. We have to drop these off at my friend's house, and we still have to get our stained glass art from the church lawn.

"We'll be in touch," Pete said with a wave.

"Thanks, man," Heath said as he extended his hand to Pete.

"Anytime. It took us a few tries to settle into our careers too," Pete said as they shook hands.

Heath watched Tessa heading for the exit. "Yeah, let's hope she doesn't end up working for the CIA before she figures it out."

Few people in Freedom knew that Pete O'Rourke spent twenty-five years as a CIA operative before coming home to be the friendly neighborhood insurance agent.

Pete chuckled. "I don't think we have to worry about her."

"It's a good thing. See ya," Heath said as he pushed through the crowded bakery following Tessa.

She waited for him on the snowy sidewalk with the bag tucked under her arm. "Let's go. I'm freezing."

Tessa's steps were two for each one of his as they headed to the art display the next block over. Tessa grabbed the lantern, while the art teacher, Mrs. Gilbert, showed Heath how to properly handle Claire's delicate piece.

"Now, remember to pick it up by the metal rods when you take it out of the case," Mrs. Gilbert repeated.

Heath looked at the big plywood box made to fit the exact dimensions of the art. "Thanks for your help. I'd hate to mess this up," Heath said as he gently lifted it using the handle.

Mrs. Gilbert clasped her hands and tucked them under her chin. "Claire is a blessing. I'm so glad to have her in my class. She made this case herself just for transporting it to and from the exhibit."

Heath couldn't help but be impressed—not only by her handiwork, but by her dedication to protecting something she cared about. He'd built his life around protecting people, places, and things, and he knew a job well done when he saw it.

"She's amazing," Tessa echoed. "Everything she touches turns to art."

Mrs. Gilbert wrapped an arm around Tessa's shoulders. "You're a gift too. I've had Claire in some of my classes before, but she's so much happier since she met you. You know, I worry about her." The older lady's tone had shifted from upbeat optimism to the gentle nurturing tone of a mother.

Tessa squeezed the woman in return. "I'll take care of her."

"I hate that she couldn't be here tonight. She was so excited about it," Mrs. Gilbert said.

"Me too, but we're on our way to see her now. We'll make sure she's doing okay."

Tessa's use of *we* had Heath a little stumped. There wasn't much he could do to help Claire, especially since he didn't know anything about her or what kind of help she might need.

Heath and Tessa said good-bye to Mrs. Gilbert and started the long trek toward Heath's SUV on the other side of town.

Tessa shivered. "Remind me again why we parked so far away."

"You're carrying a tiny lantern and a bag of scones." Not that Claire's art piece was heavy, but he felt as if he were carrying the Mona Lisa or something equally important.

"Speaking of being out of shape, Claire goes hiking with her dad almost every week on his day off," Tessa said. "It's really important to her."

Heath narrowed his eyes at his sister. It seemed like a random comment that left him confused and, despite his better judgment, curious. "Okay. Is there a reason I need to know that?"

"Her dad can't come home this week, and she's really bummed about it. She loves hiking around Freedom Ridge. That's when she gets the inspiration for her paintings."

"Okay. I'm still not sure why you needed me to know."

Tessa shrugged. "Just thought I'd mention it."

Heath pondered what Tessa had said while she pointed out turns leading them to Claire's house. He could ask Claire if she'd like to hike with him this week while her dad was gone, but would he be overstepping? The constant fear that he'd push too far and scare her away was looming, and it was the last thing he wanted to do.

His infatuation with Claire was growing by the

minute, but he stomped it down with every breath. He didn't know the first thing about working into Claire's heavily guarded circle of trust, and while the realization should have scared him off, he found himself unable to turn away and forget about her.

"It's about a mile up this road on the left," Tessa said as they turned onto a quiet street just outside of town.

He'd need more than a mile to figure out what to do about his infatuation with Claire.

6

CLAIRE

*C*laire stared at the gallery of images on her computer. She'd photographed every painting before sending them to Art and Soul, but the old scenes weren't sparking anything new for her.

She let her head fall back onto the couch. Surely, she remembered something from the hikes with her dad that she hadn't painted yet. She usually chronicled visual memories of worthy scenes during the hikes, and if she passed by it without studying the lighting, background, and details of the setting, it was lost to her memories forever.

Shoving the laptop onto the couch beside her, she stood and paced the living room. She could go out on her own, but the mere thought almost paralyzed her. Not only was she terrified of venturing out alone, but she'd heard stories of hikers getting lost on the ridge. Those news headlines usually had a fatal report followed by a reminder to hike safely.

Claire nervously rubbed her thumbnail over the ridges of her teeth and looked at the clock. It was almost 9:30 at night. Her mom would still be awake. She could stay the night at her parents' place and get some rest knowing help was only steps away if something bad happened.

But something bad wasn't always waiting to happen. Why did she focus on the bad to the point where the mere thought crippled her?

She huffed and stalked toward the kitchen, unsure of what she'd do when she got there. She couldn't go running home every time she got scared, but she wanted to. Relief from the stress and worry was a few minutes' drive away, and it was tempting.

Claire propped both hands on the kitchen sink and tried to breathe through the anxiety attack that was clawing its way up her throat. She looked up at the small picture window above the sink. The curtains were closed as usual. Shutting herself away from the world was the safest thing to do, but the walls were closing in.

"Lord, I'm scared," Claire whispered into the quiet kitchen. "I'm scared, and I don't know why. This is so silly. Why am I this way? Please, please calm my heart." She rubbed a hand over her face and sucked in a gulp of air before closing her eyes and pushing it out with ballooned cheeks.

Her heel tapped wildly on the floor, bouncing at a rate that could compete with her heart. "Should I go to Mom's? Should I…" She swallowed hard. "Should I call Heath?"

Claire liked Heath. As much as she tried to tell herself he was just another guy who wouldn't put up with her neurotic fears, a glimmer of hope bloomed in her chest. What if he was different? She adored Tessa, and Heath had been so kind. He'd know what to do. Security was his job.

Claire might have a small crush on him, but she'd never be bold enough to do anything except hide away her feelings. That was what she did. She hid from life. How much more could Jake have stolen from her four years ago?

Jake had turned everything upside down. Claire had been eager to date in college, hoping to one day have a husband and start a family. Turns out, she'd been too eager and trusted the wrong man.

Tears began to swim in her eyes as the hope died. She was so far removed from any kind of relationship that she didn't know where to begin. She'd shunned every inkling of feelings with her fear for so long. How could she open her heart to that kind of trust? The first man she'd trusted had hurt her.

Three quick knocks on the door made Claire

jump and turn, bumping her knee against the cabinet door. "Ouch." She tried to whisper, but the sting in her knee shot up her leg.

"It's me!" Tessa yelled from outside.

Claire took a deep breath and headed for the door. She'd forgotten Tessa was stopping by after the tree lighting tonight. With a hand on the knob, Claire checked her reflection in the small mirror on the wall. Red eyes and dark circles. Great.

She stretched her mouth into a grin. If she started smiling from ear to ear, Tessa would know something was up in a hurry, so the simple upturn of her mouth would be best.

When Claire opened the door, Tessa stood shivering on the porch with Heath behind her holding the case Claire had made to protect the stained glass.

At the sight of Heath's friendly face, her own feigned expression softened into something simpler and genuine. She was also keenly aware that she hadn't fixed her hair today, opting to twist it up into a wet knot high on her head. Without thinking, she brushed a hand over the stray strands hoping to tame them.

She stepped out of the doorway. "Come in. Thanks so much for this. How was the tree lighting?"

"It was fun. I'm bummed that you didn't get to come. Everyone loved your stained glass art."

Heath lifted the box. "Where do you want me to put this?"

Claire pointed to a spot against an empty wall. "Just leave it there, please. I'll move it later."

She watched as he lowered the box to the floor as if it were a sleeping newborn. Seeing him take such care of something she valued warmed her heart. When she looked back at Tessa, Claire knew she'd been caught daydreaming.

Tessa narrowed her eyes at Claire, and she knew her friend had seen through her thinly veiled anxiety.

"I forgot the pastries in your car. Can you grab them, please?" Tessa asked Heath without breaking her stare with Claire.

"Sure."

Once Heath was out the door, she felt a spark of shame. Tessa was her good friend—the best—and Claire had overlooked her kindness in favor of admiring Tessa's brother.

"Hey, what's up?" Tessa's tone was soft and caring, and her hand rested gently on Claire's arm.

Maybe she hadn't been caught. "Nothing."

"You look like you've been crying. I can send Heath home and stay the night with you if you need company."

"No, no. I'm really okay. Thanks for checking on

me though. I was just sitting around worrying over nothing."

Tessa's stare was unwavering as she studied Claire's face for sincerity. "Are you sure you don't know of anyone who would try to hurt you, like with the car last night?"

"I'm really sure. You know why I'm so scared all the time. I don't think Jake would come after me." Though every time she thought of the possibility, it gained credibility.

"I know. I'm just checking. I'd feel better if you let Heath update your security system."

"I—"

"Just think about it," Tessa said in a rush as Heath stepped back inside.

He handed a brown sack to Tessa, who passed it straight to Claire. "Goodies for you. Jan said she sent you the best."

Claire opened the bag and peered inside. Thick pastries wrapped in thin paper were piled atop each other. "Wow. Thanks so much."

"I wanted to make sure to get something you'd like," Tessa said.

Claire crumpled the top of the paper bag in her hand. Tessa had a good point about the security system. If Claire had Heath do some updates, she might feel a little safer and get some peace. But she had no idea how to admit that she needed help. "I was thinking about what you suggested," she whispered.

Tessa stepped closer and whispered back, "About Heath and the security system?"

Claire nodded.

"He won't bite," Tessa assured with an easy grin.

"I know. Thanks for always looking out for me," Claire whispered.

When she looked over Tessa's shoulder, Heath was studying one of Claire's paintings in the living room, kindly giving her a chance to talk to Tessa privately.

"Would you like some coffee?" Claire asked loud enough that Heath would know he was included in the invitation.

"Decaf?" Tessa asked. "I had way too much hot chocolate tonight."

Claire looked to Heath.

"I'll take a cup of decaf too." He pointed to one of half a dozen paintings on the wall in the living room. "You care if I check these out?"

Heat warmed Claire from the inside out. Did he truly like her paintings, or was he bored and just being nice? "Look all you want."

It had been ages since she'd welcomed anyone other than Tessa and her parents into her home, but she felt at ease with Heath in her safe space.

Tessa joined Heath in the living room while

Claire brewed coffee. Maybe by the time she had their drinks ready, she'd relax enough to ask Heath for help.

"Cream or sugar?" Claire asked from the kitchen.

"Both for me," Tessa said. "I'll fix it." She walked into the kitchen and headed straight for the creamer and sugar just as she'd done every time she'd visited.

Heath stepped up to the tall bar in the kitchen and leaned on the counter. "I'll take it black. Thanks."

Claire handed him the warm drink and pried her gaze away when he lifted the cup to his lips. Geez, she had to stop staring. "You want to sit by the fire?" she asked.

"I call the recliner!" Tessa shouted as she threw a tablespoon of sugar into her coffee and dashed into the living room to claim her spot.

Claire laughed. It seemed happiness came easier when her friend was around. "Does she think we're going to fight her for it?"

"She's the youngest. She had to fight for everything," Heath said.

Claire picked up her own cup and walked slowly into the living room. "Can't say I know what that's like."

"You don't have brothers and sisters?"

She shook her head. "It's just me."

Tessa toed off her boots and tucked her feet into

the comfy recliner near the fireplace. "I can't imagine life without Heath, Rachel, and Cora."

Claire sat on the side of the couch closest to Tessa and Heath took the seat next to her, leaving plenty of room on his other side. Did he want to sit close to her? Did she want him sitting close to her? She was always aware of the space around her, and any breach in that perimeter set off automatic alarms in her head. Thankfully, she didn't feel that panic. Even when sitting beside her, he left a barrier of space between them.

"It can get lonely. I always had my mom growing up. She stayed home with me, and Dad was on the road. She's the one who taught me to paint. It was her hobby."

"It's more than a hobby for you. You took it to the next level," Tessa said.

Claire shrugged. "Do what you love, and you'll never work."

Tessa sighed. "One of these days I'm going to figure out what I'm supposed to do. You two are lucky."

Claire turned to Heath. He did seem to love his job, but she knew so little about what he actually did. "What's the name of your security firm?" she asked.

"Got Your Six Security. It's what I did for the Marines—Intelligence and recon—so it only seemed natural to continue in the security field when I got out."

Got your six. She knew the saying, and it was fitting for his business.

Claire held her hands wrapped around the warm mug of coffee and stared into the dark depths. "I was thinking... Actually, Tessa mentioned it. I'd like... I wanted to ask if you could maybe update my home security system."

By the time she'd finished her stammering spiel, she was convinced she'd made a fool of herself. She had no idea if he even did home security systems. He might be a bodyguard for rich and famous people or only work for big companies.

His response was quick and sure. "I can take care of that. It'll be easy. When do you want it?"

Claire hadn't really thought this through. "I'm not sure. I guess whenever you have the time."

She tore her gaze from her coffee and braved a look at him. Heath rubbed a hand over his mouth as he looked around the room. "Two exits?"

"Yes."

"Can you show me around a little bit? I need to make some notes. I can set it up tomorrow."

Claire's eyes widened. "Tomorrow? On a Saturday?"

"It doesn't have to be tomorrow, but I'm free tomorrow."

"I just didn't realize you worked on weekends."

Heath looked around some more. "Not on Sundays, usually. But I don't have any other plans. I'd like to get it installed so you feel more secure here, especially after what happened last night."

Claire bit the inside of her lip. The car that had almost hit them was still a mystery to her. "Thanks. I'll be here tomorrow if you're sure it's okay."

"Not a problem at all," Heath assured.

Tessa whooped. "Finally! I'll sleep better knowing Heath is setting you up. He's the best."

"How do you know? You haven't ever talked to my clients."

"I remember when you saved Joanna," Tessa quipped. "She told me what you did."

"That wasn't really me. It was Aiden," Heath said.

"You put a tracker on her phone, and Aiden and the police knew where to find her."

"A tracker?" Claire asked.

"It was a tracer on her phone. She asked me to do it because she knew she might find herself in trouble, and she wanted there to be a way to find her."

"Was that easy?" Claire questioned.

"Oh, yeah," Heath said lightheartedly. "The easiest trick in the book."

"Could you do that for me?"

"Sure. I can do it now. Do you have your phone?"

Claire stood and retrieved her phone from the

kitchen. She handed it to him, easily trusting him with the private information inside. "The code is 0697."

"Who do you want to be able to see where you are and get the emergency alert if you send it?" he asked.

"Oh, I hadn't thought about that. Maybe my mom?"

"What about Heath?" Tessa asked. "He doesn't have to look at it all the time, but it'd be nice if you could get in touch with him. He could send help quickly."

Heath looked at Claire as if waiting for her answer. Did she even have the option to assign him as her contact? They hardly knew each other, but he did seem like someone she'd want to be able to call if she found herself in trouble.

She hesitated, pondering her options.

"Why don't you show me around while you think about it?" he asked.

"Okay." Yes. She needed time. She knew what she wanted to say, but the fear of actually speaking threatened to choke her.

Heath stood, leaving her phone and his drink on the coffee table. Claire rose to her feet and pointed toward the short hallway leading to the back part of the house. "The living room and kitchen make up the front of the house. There's two bedrooms, a bathroom, a laundry room, and my studio in the back."

Claire led Heath around, very aware of his close proximity. Her house wasn't one of those tiny homes her mom liked to watch people renovate on HGTV, but it was definitely meant to be a starter home. The hallway was only wide enough for them to walk single file, and having her back to any other man would have dredged up fears and panic.

She opened the door of the studio and stepped inside. Heath followed her, studying every inch of the room.

"This is where I work." She pointed to the door she usually kept open for ventilation. "This is the only other door."

"I don't think I've ever seen an artist's studio before," Heath said. A hint of wonder laced his tone.

"They're usually messy," Claire admitted. "Mine is no exception."

Heath's attention turned from the canvases and paint supplies to her. His warm brown eyes gave his expression a measure of softness that loosened the tightness in her shoulders.

"I don't know how you can make those awesome paintings from nothing," he said.

Her cheeks heated, and a smile tugged her lips. He had the stance and confidence of a man who seemed like he was capable of anything, yet he was impressed by her work—the very heart and soul of her passion.

"Thanks. It comes easy now. I've been painting since I was young."

Heath rubbed a hand over his mouth, and she was drawn to the source of the soft scratching sound of his fingers against the stubble on his jaw.

"Tessa mentioned you like to hike."

Claire nodded, not trusting her voice while his gaze peered so deeply into her.

"With your dad?" he finished.

"Yeah. When he's home."

"Tessa mentioned he isn't home for your hike this week. I could take you somewhere tomorrow if you wanted."

Claire stared at him, her face void of any emotion that churned inside her. She'd love to hike tomorrow, but she'd only known Heath for two days.

"Yes! Hiking sounds like a great idea. Doesn't it?" Tessa said as she burst into the studio. Her nose crinkled, and she squinted. "Your studio stinks. How do you work in here?"

Claire chuckled. Leave it to Tessa to break up the uncomfortable pause. "It's turpentine. I usually work with the door and windows open."

"That's good to know," Heath said as he typed on his phone. "I think I have a program that would be good for you. It's simple but secure."

The weight on Claire's chest lifted. "Great."

"But I have some other comparable programs. Would you like to go over a few of them?" he asked.

"No. You just pick one." Claire caught herself at the end of the sentence. She'd almost added that she trusted him. Did she? Could she? It was hard to believe Heath, who seemed so genuine, could ever do her any harm.

Heath's mouth tugged up on one side. He was clearly pleased with her faith in him. "What time do you want me here?"

"Oh, I get up around six in the morning. Any time after seven would be great."

"I'll be by around eight. It shouldn't take more than a few hours to set up the security system. I can send you a quote when I get back to my computer tonight."

"Okay. What's a price range I should expect?"

Heath pulled out his phone and typed for a moment before showing her a document with line items and a bolded price at the bottom. "It should be somewhere around this."

Claire nodded. "That's not bad. Thanks."

Tessa yawned and stretched her arms over her head. "I need to hit the hay, folks."

Heath chuckled. "Let's get you home, Cinderella."

"I've always thought of myself as more of a sleeping beauty," Tessa noted as she led the way back through the hall to the living room. "So, are you two hiking tomorrow?"

Claire turned to Heath, who looked at her expectantly.

"I'd really like to," Claire said. Oddly enough, the admission wasn't followed by uncertainty or embarrassment.

Heath smiled, revealing a peek of his white teeth. "We can go after I install the system."

Claire turned to Tessa. "You want to come?"

"Oh no," Tessa said, wagging her finger in the air. "I'm more of an indoorsy person."

"Okay then," Claire said, suddenly brimming with joy. She was going to get to explore this week, even if her dad couldn't come home.

"Where do you want to go?" Heath asked.

That was something she should have thought of sooner. "Oh, my dad usually picks the locations. Do you have anything in mind?"

"My friend Aiden is out of town. He has a nice cabin by Freedom Lake, and the view is great. There are some trails around the lake that are still passable. How does that sound?"

"Perfect." It truly did sound ideal. It had been a while since she'd painted a series with a lake in it, and she couldn't recall ever going to Freedom Lake.

"See you in the morning," Heath said as he headed for the door where Tessa waited impatiently wrapped in her coat. "I'll finish setting up your tracker tomorrow after you decide on who you want to link your location to."

"Bye!" Tessa sang. "I'll talk to you later." Her smile was bright and mischievous like a kid who'd just gotten her way.

Claire stood in the doorway to say her good-byes. There wasn't even a hint of her earlier anxiety.

When the headlights from Heath's SUV disappeared down the road, Claire stepped back inside and closed the door, double locking it and activating the current security system. With her nightly ritual complete, she rested her back against the door and released a long, therapeutic breath. She needed to get some sleep before her hike tomorrow, but excitement stirred in her middle.

It wasn't a date, but she wished it were. If her life was different, she'd hope there could be something more than casual acquaintance between Heath and herself.

But this was her life, and the energy that lingered after tonight's visit was cause for hope.

Maybe her life could be different.

*H*eath parked in front of Claire's house the next morning and scanned the small yard. Everything seemed quiet and undisturbed. Her place was far enough from the bustle of downtown to stay untouched by tourism. On the other hand, it was farther from law enforcement headquarters.

He didn't want to dwell on the downside. There probably wasn't anything to worry about. The sidewalk incident might have been a random person being negligent. If Claire didn't think she was being targeted, he shouldn't either.

He went to the back of the Tahoe first and gathered the things he'd need this morning, reminding himself this was just a job.

Well, it was a job until the hike. He intended to pull out all the stops to make sure Claire had a good time later. He hadn't specified that it was a date, but he hoped the afternoon would lead to an opportunity to ask for one by name.

The beginning of December brought the surge of winter weather that attracted tourists to the ridge, but Heath decided against adding another layer until it came time to hike. He'd be working inside, and he hoped Claire offered him another cup of coffee to warm his insides while he installed the system.

He rapped two quick knocks on the door and checked his watch. Right on time.

The door opened, and Claire greeted him with a lazy smile. Her hair was gathered into a low ponytail that fell over one shoulder, and she wore a beige knit sweater that hugged her curves.

Heath cleared his throat. He saw her just last night, but he'd forgotten the extent of her beauty. He wouldn't be needing that cup of coffee. The blood in his veins boiled when she looked his way.

"Good morning," she said cheerily with a tilt of her head.

"Good morning."

Claire stepped out of the doorway, welcoming him in. "I made coffee. You want some?"

He put the equipment on an empty sofa table and removed his thick coat. He needed to cool down about ten degrees before ingesting the hot drink. "Sure."

"Where do you need to start?"

"I'll be all over the place. This shouldn't take long."

Claire clasped her hands in front of her. "I'll get that coffee and stay out of your way."

When she disappeared into the kitchen, Heath got to work. The sooner he got the security system installed, the more time he'd have to hike with her. There were a few times throughout the morning that he caught himself sneaking glances at her as she lounged on the couch with a book. He'd never had a problem focusing before, especially when it came to his job, but today, Claire provided a tempting distraction.

He wasn't sure what he'd gotten himself into, but the morning consisted of stomping down wayward thoughts of Claire. He'd successfully push his curiosities aside only for her to appear in the doorway of the room he was working on and offer him a glass of water. Once, she hung around and asked a few questions about what he was doing. He answered on autopilot, hoping the talk about work would focus him on the task.

The shyness he'd seen in her before seemed to be slowly dissipating. Her words were few, but he heard the kindness in each one. It was impossible not to overhear her phone conversations with her mother and Tessa in the next room.

Tessa hadn't made a secret of pushing him toward Claire last night. The drive home had consisted of Tessa's hopes that the hike went well alongside her warnings to tread lightly with her friend.

If only he knew how careful he needed to be and why. Claire didn't seem interested in a romantic relationship, but he didn't know her well enough to be sure about anything.

When he was finished with the installation, he stepped into the living room where she sat with a laptop. She looked up at him with an easy smile, and his heart did a flip in his chest. Good grief, how was he supposed to keep a level head when she looked at him like that?

"You're all set up."

She pushed the laptop to the side and stood. "Great. Thanks so much."

"Can I set some things up on your phone?" he asked.

"Sure."

She handed it to him, and he moved to stand shoulder-to-shoulder with her so she could see what he was doing. He connected the app and let her fill in her information before he took her through the basics.

He went to the equipment on the table and found the bracelet. "I need to link this too. It's an emergency bracelet. If you want to silently call for help, this sends me an alert with your location.

"Wow. This is nice. I feel better already."

"Can I put my number in your phone?" he asked.

"That would be great." Claire didn't look at him as he added his contact information. Her cheeks blushed a faint pink. "I hope I don't need to call you with any problems, but I'm sure I'll mess up activating it or trying to deactivate it at least once."

Heath handed the phone back to her. "You can call me for anything. Don't hesitate." He truly didn't want her to second-guess calling him, but he was afraid it would be the case. He secretly hoped he'd be getting her number by the end of the day.

"Thanks. I'm glad you know so much about this. I hardly know how to use my computer."

"You just work better with paint and canvas," Heath assured. "I've been working with this stuff for years, so it's second nature. I worked in intelligence for the Marines first."

"Tessa told me about that. It sounds interesting. My life is so far removed from anything you'd do as a Marine."

Heath swallowed the hard lump in his throat. He'd enjoyed working with the Marines. He'd always thought it was what he was born to do, until his career imploded with that building in Kandahar.

That was all it took. One tiny mention that sent

him back to that big mistake had his mood sinking like a rock.

Claire fidgeted, shifting her weight from one foot to the other. "Well, I'll pack us some sandwiches for lunch."

"Thanks. Can I use your restroom?"

"Sure. It's around that corner."

Heath closed himself in the small guest bath and tried to forget about Kandahar. It was over, and Freedom, Colorado was thousands of miles away from that mistake.

That didn't change what happened, and he knew it.

His phone dinged with a text, and he grasped for the distraction. Using the restroom was just an excuse to get his head together before spending the rest of the afternoon with Claire. He wanted to be focused and alert when he was with her.

Tessa: How is she?

Heath gripped his hair by the roots and tugged. Everything about Claire was different, and it was enough to send his awareness into overdrive. His sister should be asking, "How's the date going?" but instead, she's checking on her friend like she was sick or injured.

Heath: We need to talk.

Tessa: About what? Is she okay?

Heath: She's fine. I just don't know why you're acting like this or why she's so scared all the time.

When Tessa didn't respond right away, Heath took his time piddling around the restroom. Maybe Tessa was typing out some long explanation.

His phone dinged while he was washing his hands, and he dried them off on the hand towel in a rush.

Tessa: Something happened to her. It's not my place to talk about, but she has reasons. Just be patient.

Heath sucked in a deep breath and typed the last text as he stepped out of the restroom.

Heath: I can do that.

It looked like he'd be left in the dark a little longer. In the meantime, all he could do was tread lightly and not do anything to make Claire uncomfortable. He resolved himself to unwavering patience and walked into the kitchen where she waited.

She looked over her shoulder with a soft smile. "You like ham or turkey?"

"Either. I'll eat anything."

Claire looked back to the sandwiches she was wrapping in paper towels. "Does that really come from eating bad food when you were overseas?"

He rested his back against the counter beside her and chuckled. "Nah. I've never been a picky eater.

Mostly because my sisters used to eat all the good stuff and pass me the things they didn't want."

"Aw, man. That's sad."

"Not at all. They didn't want meat and veggies—my favorites."

Claire's smile widened, and Heath's gaze stayed locked on that happy expression.

"You're a good brother."

Heath rested his hands on the edge of the counter behind him. "How do you know?"

"Tessa thinks the world of you. And I heard you encouraging her at Valentino's the other night. It's great that she has someone to support her."

"She has more than just me. Our family is tight, and we can't have our little runt turning into a wanderer."

Claire continued to grin as she tucked the bagged sandwiches into a small thermal cooler.

"All joking aside, Tessa is great, and I know she'll figure out what she wants to do with her life. She just needs to be patient. The Lord has a plan for her. She just doesn't know what it is yet."

Claire's head jerked up, and her gaze locked with his. "I think that's true too."

"I guess I'll be her cheerleader while she waits."

Claire grinned. "I'll do that too. I've been struggling with what I can do to help her."

Heath followed Claire to the front door. "I'm glad

she has you. I've always worried Tessa would fall in with the wrong crowd one day."

Claire adjusted her thick coat and tugged her ponytail from the collar. "I don't think you have to worry. She's been the one keeping me in line, reminding me to keep my faith."

Heath tugged on his own coat, trying not to read too much into the mystery in her words. "Thanks for that. Let's practice activating this new system."

Claire went through the motions and pressed the buttons at the right time without any reminders.

"You did a great job arming the system," Heath said as he tugged on his boots and followed her to the SUV.

"I can't believe I got it right on the first try."

Heath reached to open the passenger door of his Tahoe for her, but her attention darted to her Jeep and back.

"Do you want to drive separately?" he asked, realizing too late this was one of those situations when she might need space.

"Um, no. I'll ride with you if that's okay."

He gestured for her to step up into the SUV. "Be my guest."

When she was settled inside, Heath walked around the front of the vehicle and took his place behind the wheel. He pressed a few buttons on the screen in the dash, pulling up the navigation system.

"This is where we're going. You can track our progress as we go. Tessa already knows where we're going in case something happens."

Claire visibly relaxed into her seat. "Thanks. I haven't been alone with a…many people in a while."

A man. She was going to say she hadn't been alone with a man in a while. Heath knew it as surely as he knew the sun rose in the east and set in the west.

His grip tightened on the wheel as he tried to contain the whirlwind of emotions that swirled in his head.

Anger, fear, pity—it was all there, wrapped into one knot he didn't know how to unravel. He would push his assumptions aside for today, but if he was right about Claire's wariness, he'd already pushed things too far too fast by asking her to go out alone with him today. Tessa must have really said something nice about him for Claire to have agreed to this.

She peered closer to the screen. "Where is it?"

"My friends Aiden and Joanna Clark have a place on Freedom Lake. There's a trail that starts near their cabin that leads around part of the waterfront."

Claire sat back in her seat, and Heath risked a glance at her. That smile was back, and the light in her eyes could lure a sailor to the jagged rocks.

"It's been a long time since I painted a water scene."

"Well, get ready because this spot is top notch. I told them that if they ever decide to sell, I want to be first in line to buy it."

Claire slowly wrapped her fingers over each other in her lap. "I couldn't afford lakefront property. Real estate around here is expensive."

"Tell me about it. But it's..." Heath cleared his throat and stopped his train of thought before he blurted out that it was the perfect place to start a family—the real reason he was drawn to the property. "It's a great place. You'll see."

"I trust you."

Heath tried not to read too much into the words, but his chest constricted anyway. What would trust mean to Claire? She'd trusted him with her safety and security already. Now she was trusting him to take her somewhere special so she could paint scenes to sell in town.

Trusting him with those things didn't mean she was anywhere near ready to trust him with her heart.

8

CLAIRE

*C*laire leaned forward in her seat as Heath turned into a short drive. The quaint cabin was framed by the silvery-blue lake behind it. "This place is gorgeous," she whispered in awe.

"What'd I tell you?"

His knowing smirk pulled a smile from her own lips.

"I know exactly why you'd want first dibs on this place."

Heath picked up his hat from the center console and slipped it on his head. "Is this like the places you go with your dad?"

She slid her hands into her gloves. "Not exactly, but I'm not complaining."

"Stay right there," Heath said as he opened the door and darted out into the cold.

Claire waited as he jogged around the front of the SUV. "Well, I'll be," she whispered as Heath reached her door and opened it.

Accepting his offered hand, she choked out a quick "Thank you." Opening doors for women must be his thing.

Granted, she scared off every man who thought to look her way. They were usually the bold, cat-calling kind, but they tucked tail and ran as soon as she panicked like a cornered animal at the slightest hello.

Heath grabbed their backpacks and the small cooler of food and drinks from the back. "I have a key. You need anything from inside before we head out?"

She slid the small pack onto her back and looked around. "I think I'm ready."

Heath closed the back hatch and jerked a thumb toward the lake. "Let's go."

They walked around the front of the cabin, and the view of the lake widened. Claire found herself at a loss for words. She never missed the beauty of nature, but this was unlike anything she'd seen before. Snow covered the perimeter of the lake and scattered into a thin sheet of ice at the edges. Evergreens draped in shimmering white reflected on the glassy surface, and the vivid blue sky was streaked with white clouds.

The path ran along the lake in front of a row of cabins that sat back on the slight rise away from the lake. They'd barely made it past the third cabin when she asked to stop. Heath waited patiently as she studied the angle of the sun, the shadows, and the variations in color. After she'd spent a minute committing the scene to memory, she pulled out her camera and captured a few shots. Julia at the art gallery would have a fit for these paintings. If Claire took her time on the hike today, she could make it into a two-week series.

Heath was quiet throughout most of the hike, but every time she snuck a peek in his direction, she found him already looking back at her. Her cheeks heated every time their gazes met, despite the cold wind. Was he enjoying this, or had he only volunteered to escort her out of pity?

She'd given up hope of finding a man to share her life with when her fears had made it nearly impossible to start a relationship. Once, she'd been a shy girl with a dreamer's heart. She'd wanted—and foolishly believed—an epic love story waited in her future, but a gaping fear had swallowed those hopes long ago.

Walking beside Heath along the bank of Freedom Lake provided an imagery she couldn't deny. She wanted this kind of companionship with a man, but even thinking about the next step for them was scary.

First dates turned into second dates, and second dates turned into third dates. At some point, Heath would expect things to move forward, and that's where her hope died. She'd kissed men she'd dated in college, but the thought of intimacy sent her mind reeling back to the night a man she'd thought she'd known had nearly taken her innocence.

Claire's breathing quickened at the memory. The strong hands weighed heavy on her wrists, cracking the small bones that pressed into the jagged rocks. His hot breath smelled of spiced rum as his short, rough beard scraped her lips and chin. His teeth scraped hers until the taste of blood filled her senses.

The panic and the fear mingled, turning her lungs into stone. That wasn't what a kiss was supposed to be.

"Hey, you okay?" Heath asked beside her.

No, she wasn't okay. She was messed up, and now she couldn't even think about something as sweet as a kiss without hurling herself into a panic attack. "Yeah." Who was she kidding? That didn't sound convincing at all.

"Tell me about painting. How do you do it?"

Claire lifted her chin to look at him. "What do you mean?"

"I don't know. Tell me what you love about it."

Bless him. He was trying to take her mind off the bad that was threatening to strangle her by thinking about the things she loved. "It's the colors."

When she didn't elaborate, Heath chuckled. That deep, comforting sound wrapped around her like a blanket on a cold night.

"You must see something I can't. It's mostly white out here," he said, gesturing to the snow-covered scene.

"No, there's more than white here. Even small variations of color have an impact. Shading, depth, and hue work together to make the flat image look like a three-dimensional scene."

"I guess I understand."

"Did you know we associate colors with feelings?"

"Like, red and black are anger or danger?" he asked.

"Not exactly. Have you ever noticed that restaurants often have a warm color palette? Reds and oranges can provoke hunger."

"No way."

"Yes way. Depending on the setting, yellow can evoke happiness or confusion."

Heath nodded slowly as he stared at the path ahead. "I'm definitely confused right now," he said with a deep chuckle.

Claire shrugged. "It's true. Colors can be complimentary, meaning they pair well with other colors—those that are directly opposite on the color wheel."

Heath raised a hand. "Hold up. What's a color wheel?"

Claire laughed, and happiness bubbled in her chest. "Don't think too hard about it, but next time you walk into a room dominated by a certain color, think about the way it makes you feel."

"I can't promise anything, but I'll try." He stopped and looked around. "You want to stop here for lunch?"

Claire turned in a full circle. The small, flat area was shaded by trees with a clear view of the lake. "Looks perfect to me."

Heath pulled out their sandwiches and stopped. "I'd like to bless the food."

Claire bit her bottom lip and nodded.

He lowered his chin. "Lord, thank You for guiding us here today. Thank You for this food, and I pray You'll bless it and the hands that prepared it. In Jesus's name I pray. Amen."

Claire lifted her chin and accepted the sandwich he offered her. He couldn't have known it, but she often prayed that God would bless her hands. The same hands that prepared this food painted scenes of God's creation, and she wanted her art to always reflect the Lord's gift of nature and goodness.

They sat on a slope a few feet from the edge of the lake and ate in silence. She snuck glances at him and always caught him looking back. Each time, he averted his gaze only to look back again a few moments later.

Heath cleared his throat. "I've been thinking about colors, like you said. Do you have a favorite color?"

Claire didn't have to think long before the answer painted itself on her thoughts. "Midnight blue. You?"

Heath leaned forward, propping his elbows on his knees. "I really like the color of your eyes."

Claire laughed, and the joyful sound filled the quiet forest at their backs. "What a line!"

Heath was trying to contain his smile. "Let me finish. You told me to think about how colors made me feel. That blue of your eyes reminds me of the first time my parents took me to an aquarium." He crumpled the wrapping of his sandwich in his hands. "My sisters outnumbered me, and we usually ended up doing things they'd like. There was that one time that we went to an aquarium, and even though it was something I'd picked, none of my sisters complained."

Claire rubbed a hand over her jeans, massaging some warmth into her thighs. "I don't have any memories like that. My mom stayed home with me, and Dad worked out of town five days a week. We did everything together."

"I'm glad my sisters got to do the things they loved. We're all so different that we rarely found something the whole family liked." He looked out over the lake as if he could see back in time. "Everything in the aquarium was that hazy blue. The light shining in the water, the walls, the floors—everything. I could have stayed there all day watching the sea creatures floating in the blue-tinted water. It was comforting and hypnotizing. That blue is a lot like your eyes. I think I understand what you meant when you said we associate color with feelings or moods. When I think about that color, I remember how content and happy I was that day at the aquarium."

"I think that's why people like my paintings. They're bright whites, soft blues, and natural browns and greens."

"You do a great job. I've seen some of your paintings. My mom likes the Art and Soul Gallery, and I'm pretty sure she has a few of yours."

Claire grinned. "She does. Tessa told me."

"You have a gift. It's good that you're sharing it." He tucked his wrapper into their small trash bag. "I'm glad you let me tag along today."

Claire chuckled once and playfully shoved his shoulder. "Thanks for making it sound like I could have done it without you. We both know I wasn't leaving the house this weekend."

Heath stood and began gathering their things. "You could have, but I understand your hesitation. There are dangerous animals in these woods."

She sighed. Dangers didn't only exist in the dark depths of the forest; they walked the streets disguised as friends, husbands, and employees. People could be the most dangerous predators.

A shape flashed in front of her, and she jumped. Looking up from where she sat, Heath was offering his hand to help her up.

She placed her hand in his, feeling the warmth and security as his larger hand wrapped around hers. She'd been foolishly lost in her cynical thoughts when Heath was right in front of her, proving her theory wrong. Not everyone intended to harm others. The kind, selfless man in front of her was proof enough.

When she was standing, his grip stayed tight for an extra second. "You ready to head back?" Heath asked.

"Sure." The walk back to the cabin was peaceful, and Claire relaxed as she took in the sights and scenery. She had plenty of inspiration for her paintings.

"Is this anything like your hikes with your dad?" Heath asked.

"Sort of. Our walks have gotten shorter in the last few years. He's getting older, and he needs a knee replacement."

"My dad had shoulder surgery when I was overseas. That recovery was rough on him."

"Yeah, I'm not looking forward to it. He's always been active, and I'm hoping the surgery will help if he can just take it easy during those weeks after."

"How long have you been hiking with him?"

"We started our weekly outings about a year after I got home from college. So, about three years, I guess."

"Tessa talked about that college like it was something important. Did you like it?"

It was such a simple question. Of course Heath wanted to talk about college. For anyone else, it was a normal chapter in life.

"I liked it. I learned a lot."

She *had* liked it, until her time there came to an abrupt halt.

Her short answer must have given him the hint because he didn't press her for more details about college. As they walked, she relaxed and enjoyed the beautiful scenery and his companionship.

When they could see the cabin where they'd begun, Heath pointed to the side door. "I told Aiden I'd check on things while I'm here."

Claire followed him up the steps to the porch and

waited as he unlocked the door. The inside was homey and much warmer than the frigid winter winds they'd been walking in most of the afternoon.

"I just need to check the water pipes." Heath pointed around the main floor. "There's the restroom, and you can help yourself to some water in the kitchen."

Claire tugged on the scarf around her neck, loosening it as the warmth filled her bones. Family photos rested on the mantle and sofa tables, and child's paintings and drawings hung on the refrigerator. The couple and young boy in the photos looked happy.

She'd just stepped in front of the last photo when Heath reappeared.

"Looks like everything is in order here. You ready to go?"

Claire tucked her scarf back into her collar. "Ready."

Back in Heath's SUV, Claire flipped through the photos she'd taken and told him her favorite details of each and her plans for the paintings. Today's walk had refreshed her creativity, but she also felt a lightening in her soul. She couldn't recall a time when she'd spent so much time alone with a man other than her dad, and she was proud of herself for venturing out of her comfort zone.

Truly, it was because of Heath. If she'd been out

today with anyone else, it would have been a nerve-racking day.

Heath pulled into the quiet drive at her house and parked. When he shut the SUV off, he didn't move to get out just yet.

She didn't want this day to end. Was he hesitating for the same reason?

Heath propped his elbow on the console between them and rested his chin on his fist. "Did you have fun?"

Claire grinned. "I did. Thanks for taking me."

"Anytime."

"Did *you* have a good time?" she asked.

Heath rubbed his thumb over his chin. "I did, and I'd like to do it again sometime."

Claire averted her eyes and tugged on her scarf. The heat in his stare was burning her skin. If there was ever a man she wanted to see again, it was Heath. She hadn't made it through a first date since she came back to Freedom. Maybe she'd been more relaxed today because Heath hadn't actually called it a date. There weren't as many expectations when you were hiking as there were on a date.

"You don't have to decide today, but I would like to take you out again. Can I call you?"

Heath's acknowledgment of her freedom to set the pace between them emboldened her. "I'd like that."

He handed over his phone, and she added her number to his contacts.

"And you can call me anytime—for anything." He looked out the window toward her house. "I'd like to check things out and make sure you don't have any questions about deactivating the system before I leave."

"Thanks. I'll try to remember what you told me this morning," she said as they stepped out into the cold.

She didn't wait for Heath to come around the car and open her door, and he met her with a knowing grin at the front of the SUV, taking her backpack from her and slinging it over his own shoulder.

"I'm going to check around the house," he said, pointing to the left side yard.

"I'll come with you." In truth, she wasn't ready for their time to end just yet. Going inside to the quietness that waited for her didn't sound appealing when Heath was around.

She watched as Heath's gaze traveled over everything in the side yard. There wasn't much to see except snow, trees, and a low stone wall that bordered her neighbor's lot.

Heath's steps through the thin snow were slow and sure. How could anyone question his protective instincts?

When he stepped around the corner into the

small backyard, he halted with a fist in the air at the level of his head. Leaning to the side and looking around him, Claire saw the disturbed snow that caught his attention.

Less than a second passed before Heath turned, pushing her back the way they'd come. "Run!"

The first shot rang in the air before he'd finished the command.

9

HEATH

*A*drenaline pumped through Heath's veins as he pushed Claire toward the vehicle. The shooter could be hidden anywhere in the forest surrounding the house, and they didn't have time to unlock the doors and take shelter inside.

Heath placed himself between Claire and the tree line as they ran. He said a silent prayer of thanks that Claire hadn't frozen in fear. Her fight-or-flight instincts were working just fine.

When they reached the vehicle, Heath ushered her toward the passenger side as he kept himself between her and the unseen danger. "Get down," he ordered as he closed the door and ran behind the Tahoe to the driver's side.

Inside, Heath started the engine and reversed,

and they were peeling out of Claire's driveway within seconds.

Claire panted in the seat beside him. Her head hung between her knees and her hands shielded the back of her head. "Heath, what's happening?"

An unfamiliar emotion brewed inside him. It was a mixture of rage and determination with a hint of something he couldn't place. Was that fear that had his lungs constricting?

"I don't know, but we're getting out of here." He reached over the console and rested a hand on her shoulder. "Breathe for me, Claire."

His attention darted from the road to Claire and back, watching as her back swelled with the deep inhalations.

"Where are we going?" Her voice shook with each word.

He'd been trained to think fast without making stupid decisions in a crisis. Now, he paused to sort through his coherent thoughts for the best solution. "Headquarters."

"Your work?"

"Yes. It's heavily protected."

He pressed the button on the steering wheel and gave the Bluetooth command to call Jeremiah.

The deep voice of Heath's friend answered before the end of the first ring. "Jeremiah."

"I'm with Claire Odom. We just left her house at

926 Kingsley Road. Someone opened fire on us from the perimeter. Three pistol shots. Bring in Adam and Pete. I'll call the police."

"10-4. Tracking you."

"Get eyes on that surveillance feed. I just installed it this morning."

Heath disconnected the call and phoned 911. He took the opportunity during the pauses when the dispatcher logged the emergency information to whisper assurances to Claire. This was the last thing she needed.

He ended the emergency call after the dispatcher confirmed officers were en route to the residence and at least one would be meeting them at Got Your Six headquarters to receive his and Claire's statements.

"Claire, you with me? Hang in there." Heath tightened his grip on the wheel and leveled his breathing. It wouldn't help for her to see him lose his cool right now.

"I'm okay."

The assurance was punctuated with a sob that split his heart in two. What was Claire wrapped up in that would make someone want her dead? There was no doubt that the shooter in the woods was a hired man, which meant they were at least one degree behind not-a-clue from pinpointing a suspect.

The odds weren't in their favor, but that had never stopped him before, and he didn't intend to let it now.

Heath pulled the SUV behind the building that housed headquarters. He opened the console and pulled out a small keypad where he keyed in the code to open the garage door in the back of the building.

He pulled into the open vehicle bay and closed the door behind him. They'd need to switch vehicles before leaving later.

Killing the engine, he got out and jogged around to Claire's side. He opened the door, but she remained ducked behind the dash.

"Claire, we're here."

Her body shook as she lifted her head and accepted his offered hand. Slowly, she stepped out of the vehicle and into his waiting arms. Her sobs broke free as she tucked her face into his chest.

Heath wrapped her up, holding her tighter than necessary as her tears ran out. His hand traced a continuous circle on her back while the other cradled her head. Every cell in his body was drawn to her. Every thought in his mind commanded him to protect her. And in that moment, he made a vow to guard her with his life.

"Listen, you're safe. I'm right beside you, and I won't leave you."

Claire lifted her head, revealing red-rimmed eyes and pink splotchy cheeks. "What's going on?" she cried.

Heath wiped a hand over her wet cheek, and she didn't flinch away from his touch. "I don't know yet, but I promise I'll find out."

"I have to call my mom. I call her every evening. She'll be worried if I don't." She reached for the phone in her pocket.

"Let's use a secure line. You'll need to turn that one off." Heath took her hand. "Follow me."

He thought to worry about the sudden contact, but Claire's tight grip on his hand waived any doubts about holding hers.

When they passed Jeremiah's office, Heath held up a finger indicating he'd be right back. The others should be arriving soon, and they'd need to get everyone up to speed before they had to sit down with the police.

Heath led Claire into his office and went straight to the desk. "You can sit here and use this phone. Let me secure the line."

Claire sat in the rolling chair as Heath readied the phone and handed it to her.

"I'm going to be right in the next office." He pointed to a Plexiglass window that connected his office to Jeremiah's. They usually left it open so they could talk freely instead of paging or running to each other's offices. "I'll be able to see you. Let me know if you need anything."

"Okay." Claire wiped her eyes with the backs of her hands.

Heath stopped at the door. "You want me to close this?"

Claire nodded, tucking her lips between her teeth.

After leaving her in the private room, Heath went straight to the office next door.

"What's the ETA on the others?"

"Now," said a familiar voice behind Heath, and Adam stepped in and planted his feet near the end of the desk. With his hands clasped behind him, he was ready for commands.

Heath stepped behind Jeremiah's chair and snuck a glance at Claire through the window. "Derek?"

"On his way to the scene," Jeremiah said. Derek trained search and rescue dogs, and the police would need his skills.

"Do you know who the police department is sending?" Heath asked.

"Officer Riggs. He'll be here any minute."

"Good," Heath said before risking another glance at Claire. "She's already met Ty, and that might make things easier for her."

"He responded to the attempted hit-and-run?" Adam asked.

"Yes." Heath rubbed a hand over his mouth. He could hear her crying on the phone, and it hit him square in the chest.

"He's parking now," Jeremiah confirmed.

Heath propped a hand on Jeremiah's desk and leaned toward the monitor. "Show me the surveillance. Did you make a copy for Ty? He'll want it for evidence, even if it doesn't reveal anything."

Jeremiah held up a flash drive. "Got it."

The creaking of a metal door could be heard down the hallway, and Ty entered the office. "You again?" he said, extending a hand to Heath.

"Unfortunately. It's Claire again, too."

"We still don't have any leads on that vehicle," Ty confirmed.

"Have you checked body shops around here? It should have some front-end damage from hitting that mailbox."

"Checked them last night. Nothing fit the search."

"I guess you heard what happened today."

"Shooting at Claire's place. They're securing the scene now. Derek just arrived with one of the dogs."

Heath pointed to the monitor. "Let's look at this before you get our statements."

Ty took his place on Jeremiah's other side, and they watched as Jeremiah scanned through the last few hours of video surveillance around Claire's home.

"He shows up at 14:08," Jeremiah said, pointing to a moving image near the trees in Claire's yard.

They watched in silence as the person walked up to Claire's back door. The figure wore medium gray from head to toe and had the gait of a grown man. Heath held his breath as the person on the screen tried the door, peeked through the windows, and pulled up the welcome mat.

"Please tell me she didn't hide a key under the mat," Ty said.

"We can ask her," Heath said, hoping the same thing. "She's in the other room talking to her mom, I think."

"It's not clear enough to see if he found anything," Jeremiah said.

Heath looked through the window at Claire in his office. She was still on the phone. Her elbow was propped on the desk, and she cradled her forehead in her hand.

"Has she mentioned a reason why someone would be targeting her?" Ty asked.

Heath squinted at the screen. "Not yet." He pointed at the time stamp. "When does he leave?"

Jeremiah jumped the video to 14:26. "He heads back to the forest here, but he obviously remained there, out of sight, until you showed up at 16:49."

"I'll comb through this later. Do they have any update from the scene?" Heath asked.

Ty held up his phone and walked out into the hallway.

"Conference room is on your left," Jeremiah shouted at Ty's back.

Heath rested his back against the wall where he could still see Claire. She seemed to be calming down. "Did you get in touch with Pete?" He might be an insurance agent now, but his former CIA training would come in handy.

"On his way," Jeremiah confirmed.

Ty returned less than a minute later. "Footprints leading northeast. Derek has one of his dogs on the trail."

"That'll be our best bet," Adam said.

Movement through the window caught Heath's attention. Claire was ending the call. When she lifted her head, he could see that the redness in her cheeks had faded.

Heath pushed off the wall and moved around the desk. "I'll be right back."

He knocked on his office door, and Claire opened it. She didn't look up at him, and she nervously ran her hand over her hair that remained in a tight ponytail. "Thanks for letting me use your office."

"No problem. Are you okay?"

Claire nodded. "Mom is rattled. She called Dad, and he said..." Claire paused, her attention focused on the floor. "He said he'd like to talk to you. I don't know why this is happening, but he's scared...for me. I'm scared. And my dad wanted to talk to you about your security service."

"Of course. Your protection is my top priority. We'll call him after we give our statements."

"Thank you." The words were little more than a whisper.

"Officer Riggs is here. He's the one you met Thursday night."

Claire straightened her shoulders. "I'm ready."

Heath led her to the conference room. Ty stood from his seat at the long, wooden table when they entered.

"Miss Odom, I'm Officer Riggs."

Claire shook Ty's hand. "I remember."

"Just checking. There was a lot going on when we last met."

"And that seems to be the case this time as well."

Ty gestured to a seat. "Let's talk. Can you start by recounting the events of your day?"

Heath took a seat beside Claire and listened as she told Ty everything she'd done, only looking to him twice to confirm the time.

When she finished, Ty turned to Heath. "Is that what you recall?"

"Yes. We were together most of the day. When we

left to go to Aiden and Joanna's everything was secure."

"I'll watch the video and let you know if that reveals anything that might help us. If Derek's dogs can get a direction on a vehicle, we might be able to get video surveillance from a gas station or store parking lot in town."

"That sounds helpful," Claire said. The hope in her voice was strong.

Ty slid two forms across the table to Heath and Claire. "I don't want to get your hopes up. Sometimes, evidence leads us to answers, but sometimes there isn't enough."

"I understand," Claire said as she scanned the document.

"This is for your written statement. Write down everything you told me and anything else you may remember."

Heath and Claire each picked up a pen and began writing. Heath spared no detail as he filled page after page with everything he knew that might help the police force find the man behind these attacks on Claire.

Claire finished first and handed the form to Ty.

"Thank you. I know I've already asked you this, but do you know of anyone who might want to harm you?"

Heath's hand stilled, holding the pen as he waited for Claire's answer.

When her hesitation continued, Heath's throat constricted. She knew who was behind this, but she was too scared to talk about it.

10

HEATH

*T*y leaned in and lowered his voice. "We can talk in another room if you'd like."

Heath focused on the form in front of him, silently praying Claire wouldn't take Ty up on his offer. He selfishly wanted to hear what she would say.

"No, I… I don't really know, but…" Claire wrung her hands and swallowed hard enough that Heath heard the gulp. "I was attacked four years ago. I was in college."

Heath closed his eyes. *Lord, give her words. Give her strength.*

"I went on a date with him. He was a friend of a friend, and I thought he was an okay guy." She stared down at her fingers as she twisted them. "Someone stopped him before he…"

Heath rested his forehead in his hand, and his stomach revolted.

"Were you physically injured?" Ty asked.

"I had a broken wrist and bruises on my face and neck."

Ty glanced at Heath before returning his focus to Claire. "Were the police able to identify a suspect?"

Claire nodded. "His name was Jake Barnes."

"Was there a sentencing?" Ty asked.

"He was in prison for two years. Or at least I think he was. I didn't keep up with him after I moved back to Freedom."

The plastic pen cracked in Heath's grip. She'd been attacked, abused, and violated. She couldn't have been more than twenty-one at the time.

Everything made sense. Her anxiety when they'd walked to Valentino's in the dark, her caution when they'd first met, and her reaction when he'd landed on top of her after pushing her out of the way of the wayward vehicle.

His sister's warnings made sense too. He'd spent most of his adult life praying for the safety of his sisters, but those pleas felt more vital than ever now.

Ty pointed to the form. "Could you add a little bit about that to your statement?"

Claire nodded and sat back at the table with the paper.

"Please include the city, date, and your best recollection," Ty said.

Claire stared at the form. Her shoulders sank in defeat.

Ty sighed. "I know this is hard for you, but every bit of information you can give us helps."

Claire sat down quietly, and Heath finished his statement on autopilot. Anger and adrenaline swirled in his mind until he couldn't see straight.

Heath handed his form to Ty. The look on the officer's face said he didn't like Claire's admission either.

Jeremiah stepped into the conference room. "Pete is here."

Claire was still writing, but Heath got her attention with a hand on her shoulder. "I need to talk to a friend of mine. You can find me in my office when you finish."

Claire pinched her lips together and nodded quickly. It wasn't a smile, but it was ten times better than tears.

Heath followed Jeremiah out into the hallway and to the office where their friend Pete waited.

Pete was as calm as ever. The friendly insurance agent's previous life as a secret agent provided skills that came in handy from time to time.

"Here we go," Heath said in greeting. "You in on

this one?" Pete did contract work for Got Your Six when they needed the extra manpower.

Pete shook Heath's hand. "I'm in."

"You filled him in?" Heath asked Jeremiah.

"I told him what we know."

"Good." Heath leaned back against the desk and crossed his arms over his chest. "Claire just told us something that might be a good lead. Can you get me a full profile on a Jake Barnes? There should be a criminal case from Savannah, Georgia about four years ago."

Jeremiah didn't say anything, but his pallor waned as he turned his attention to the computer.

Heath turned to Pete. "Can we use the safe house?"

"It's all yours. I haven't been there in a while, so we need to stock some things first."

"Did we get the perimeter alarm on it last month?" Heath asked.

"Yes. I just ran a test on it. All clear," Jeremiah confirmed.

Pete rested his hands on the desk. "I prayed no one would need to use it."

"I know, but I'm glad you have a place already set up."

"I guess some parts of that life won't ever die," Pete said.

Heath slapped a hand on his friend's shoulder.

"Don't give up hope. You might marry a nice woman and have a quiet retirement one day."

Pete stood to his full height. "I'm still praying. I'm not sure how I'll explain a safe house when that day comes."

"Speaking of prayer, could you say one or ten for Claire?"

"You got it. You're in my prayers too, son."

Pete's words hit Heath like a throat punch. Pete was one of the few who knew what went down in Kandahar, and he knew guilt like that never went away.

"Thanks, I appreciate it."

Pete's eyes narrowed as he studied Heath. "You sure you're the best man for this job?"

Heath crossed his arms as the challenge swelled in his chest. "Of course."

"You always this nervous?" Pete lifted his brows in question.

"No." In one word, it was the full truth. Heath lived and breathed dangerous and uncertain situations every day, but he couldn't deny that today felt different in ways he didn't want to examine under a microscope.

Pete's stare held firm. "You know what happens when we're too invested in the mission. Better men than you have forgotten their training and made hasty decisions when they got too close to the target."

"Claire is not a target. She's a person," Heath said.

Pete grinned. "I rest my case."

Heath began counting backward from twenty. Pete hadn't said anything Heath didn't already know, but it was the last thing he wanted to hear right now. It was his job to protect people, but protecting Claire was vital.

"You don't have to worry about me. I can keep my head on straight." He could argue that he was the perfect person to protect Claire. He was on high alert whenever she was around, and he couldn't take his eyes off her.

Wait. Maybe that was the point Pete was trying to make. It wasn't his job to only keep an eye on Claire. Heath's job required more than keeping the target safe. Every location the target entered had to be cleared of danger, and it had to stay that way the entire time they remained.

As for today, Heath had botched his mission before it began. One thing every personal security agent knew was that if the threat got close enough to potentially harm the protected person, you'd already failed.

Pete slapped Heath on the shoulder. "You're a good kid."

Heath laughed. "I just want to be you when I grow up."

Claire stepped into the doorway looking brighter than when they'd arrived. Her eyes were dry, and her cheeks were their usual soft ivory and also tear free.

Heath's smile faded. He'd have to talk to her dad soon, and that meant Claire might become his newest client. He'd never come close to crossing any personal boundaries with someone he worked for, and Pete's skepticism was beginning to make sense.

When Heath worked a formal event, he tempered every expression and never engaged with guests. He'd never so much as grinned while on duty. The Got Your Six handbook clearly laid out the boundaries between employees and clients. He should know. He wrote it.

Heath met Claire at the door and gestured that she should enter. "Pete, this is Claire. Claire, this is my old friend, Pete. He has a safe house, and he said we could use it."

Claire rubbed one thumb over the other. "I really have to leave my house?"

Though she'd posed a question, her tone indicated that she already knew the answer.

"I think it's best," Heath said. "Thankfully, Pete's place is almost move-in ready."

"When?" Claire asked.

"Now. Adam will take us to your house in one

vehicle. I'll stay with you while you pack some things and Pete and Jeremiah ready the location. Jeremiah will come pick us up in a different vehicle and take us to the safe house. Someone else, probably Adam, will get your bags later and bring them to us. We don't want anyone to see us leaving and think you're relocating."

Claire took a deep breath. "I guess this means I can't see my mom before we go."

"That's up to you, but I don't advise it. We don't want to lead anyone there. We'll get you a new phone so you can call them, but there needs to be minimal contact."

"I don't want that either," Claire said.

Heath was already too close. He should call her dad and tell him he wasn't the man for the job. He had about five minutes before he had to decide and call Mr. Odom.

No. Heath trusted himself to protect her with his life, and he would do everything to make sure she was protected.

"I know this will be a big change, but you'll be safe with me."

Claire's expression was unlike any he'd seen her make. Her lips were set in a thin line, and her chin was tilted up. Determination sparked in her eyes.

"Let's go."

11

CLAIRE

*C*laire stared at the clothes hanging in her closet. Heath said she needed to pack quickly, but her foggy thoughts were slowing her down. She had no idea how long she would be at the safe house.

She looked at the luggage on the bed and back to the closet before grabbing her favorite sweaters. Some were paint stained, but she needed all the comfort she could get right now.

Five minutes later, she zipped the bag and rolled it into the living room where Heath stood next to the security system panel. He poked on a laptop, entering information he read on the system.

He looked up as soon as she entered. "You ready? I'm almost finished here."

"Is it still working?" she asked.

"It's working. I'm installing remote access on the tablet so I can keep an eye on the place."

"I packed up some things I need for work too. Can I bring those?"

"Yes." His tone held none of the friendly assurances she'd grown accustomed to hearing from him. Any hint of the flirty and friendly face from earlier was gone.

"Thanks. I left the cart in the studio."

"I'll tell Adam to get it when he picks everything up later."

Claire grabbed her favorite coat from the rack by the door and saw the coat Heath had given her the night they'd met. "I'm sorry. I just realized I didn't get this back to you."

"It's okay. You needed it more."

She swung the large purse onto her shoulder. Heath suggested she pack a few necessities into something that could pass as a regular purse to use tonight. "Then I think I'm ready. Are you bringing anything?"

"I keep an emergency bag in my vehicle. Adam will bring it with your things tonight, and I'll walk him through packing some things for me later."

"When will Jeremiah be here?" Now that her things were packed, she was eager to get out of here.

"I just sent him the signal. He should be pulling in any second."

Claire peeked out the window in the living room to see a gray sedan parking out front.

Heath slid his arms into his coat and focused his attention on her. "When we walk out, don't look around. Stay beside me and walk casually to the vehicle. I'll open the door to the back seat for you and walk around to get in on the other side."

Claire nodded. She liked that he always walked her through what to do. If he hadn't said anything, she would have been tempted to make a beeline for the car while jerking her head left and right.

Heath looked at his phone. "Adam gave us the all clear." He opened the door and gestured for her to step out first. "I'm right beside you."

She stepped out onto the porch and clutched her bag on one side, stupidly hoping Heath would take her other hand. None of her thoughts and feelings made sense right now. Memories of the attack made her want to push everyone away, and she'd lived with that reality for years. Now that Heath was beside her, she ached for arms to hold her. She wanted the warmth of his presence to cradle and console her, but she was stuck in a frozen prison.

It didn't help that he'd barely looked her way since they left Got Your Six headquarters. Heath had morphed into business mode, and she missed the man who'd allowed her to cry on his shoulder.

They reached the vehicle, and Heath opened the

door for her as he said he would. She didn't look up as she slid into the seat, and he closed her into the car.

She'd been foolish to think there could be something more between Heath and herself. He'd been kind enough to install the security system and take her hiking, but it was clear that goodwill had come to an end. The phone call between Heath and her dad had severed any personal relationship they might have been kindling and replaced it with a business contract. He was being paid to stay in her presence, and that was very different from spending time with her because he wanted to.

Heath sat straight-backed in the seat beside her. "After Adam delivers your things today, you can make a list of other things you'd like to have, and he'll bring those in a few days."

"From my house?" She appreciated everything Heath and his friends were doing, but the thought of someone looking for things in her drawers made her shoulders tense.

"No, I meant from a store. If you want more paint or toiletries, he can just purchase new ones."

"Oh, thanks."

"We'll have a schedule for supply delivery, but it won't be predictable in case someone is watching. I'll let you know ahead of time so you can put together a list of things you need."

"How long do you think we'll be here?" She didn't want to sound ungrateful, but thinking about being away from her home and family made her chest ache.

"I hope it won't be long, but I don't recommend you go back until the police have found the suspect."

A hint of gentleness was back in his voice, and she'd missed it these past few hours. "Can I call my parents and Tessa?"

"We'll set up a secure line, but you'll need to keep contact to a minimum. I don't recommend you use a computer, but you're welcome to use one of mine if necessary. They're secure."

She'd need something to do during the days to keep her mind off the looming danger. Maybe she could do some painting experiments or read some books.

"Are you sure this place is safe?"

Heath didn't hesitate. "It's the safest place around. Pete is someone we can trust. He'd already implemented quite a few security measures before we installed the perimeter alarm a few weeks ago. We'll also have Derek patrolling the area regularly. He agreed to use this section of the forest to train his dogs."

"That's kind of him. I don't think I met him today."

"You didn't. He trains search and rescue dogs, and he's always happy to use Pete's land for training."

"You sure have a lot of friends with special skills."

"I do."

She waited for him to elaborate, but he didn't speak again. He'd been excited and forthcoming with information when he talked about his job earlier, but it seemed like that open book had been closed.

It was silly to be hurt by Heath's silence. He didn't owe her anything, and she'd survived without his comfort and assurance before today. Was it weird that those little pep talks had made her feel stronger? Heath knew how to build up her confidence, and she needed it now more than ever.

She spent the rest of the ride to the safe house trying to convince herself to be strong and pull her own weight. Heath was putting himself in danger to protect her, and the least she could do was make things as easy as possible while he did his job.

That meant she'd keep her emotions hidden from him. He didn't care that he was the first person she'd trusted in years, he didn't care about the gentle tug in her heart toward him, and he certainly wasn't interested in getting to know her on a romantic level.

All that was trivial compared to the threat they faced. She'd been right to keep her eyes open and her ear to the ground. Meek women like her were sitting ducks in today's world.

After ten minutes of twisting up curvy roads, Jeremiah parked the car in front of a small log cabin. It looked the same as any number they'd passed on the way in. Snow covered portions of the roof and accumulated on the edges of the porch. The little place was tucked so carefully into the evergreens that they seemed to be sheltering it with their snowy branches.

Pete stepped out and waved. It was nice to know someone was still being friendly despite the situation.

"Wait here," Heath said. "I'll come around."

Heath and Jeremiah got out, and Claire looked around the quiet patch of forest. When Heath opened her door, she looked left and right. The quaint cabin conjured images of a peaceful weekend getaway in the beautiful Rocky Mountains, and she could almost forget she was here because someone wanted to hurt her.

It didn't make sense. None of it did. Jake could have been out in the world for two years or more, and he hadn't once tried to find her. Plus, she was the one who'd been wronged, not him.

Pete greeted her at the door with a smile. "I hope you had a safe drive in."

Claire stepped inside the cabin and looked to Heath, assuming Pete was asking for a report.

Heath shook hands with Pete. "Uneventful. How's the place?"

"Everything is working. I'll send a secure email with the codes for the firearm safe, and you know where the secret exit is located."

"I appreciate it," Heath said with a curt nod.

Firearms safe? Secret exit? This wasn't the charming cabin it seemed.

Pete turned back to Claire. "Make yourself at home. Despite the circumstances, I hope you enjoy your stay here. I've tucked myself into this place a few times for a quiet weekend away. It might be small, but it has charm and comfort."

"Thank you. It's lovely," Claire said as she tilted her chin up to check out the loft. The main floor was basic with a small living area and kitchen, but she couldn't see much of what lay in the loft.

"Let me show you to your room." Pete gestured to the staircase.

"It's up there?"

"It's the only bed," Pete explained.

"Oh." The air suddenly felt thick. "Where is... Um."

"I'll be sleeping on the couch on this main floor," Heath said quickly.

"The whole time we're here?" It could be weeks,

and he would be sleeping on an uncomfortable couch.

"The whole time," he assured. "I need to be on the main floor near the clearest points of entry."

Claire bit her lips and wrung her hands. "It seems so uncomfortable. I'm sorry."

She thought she saw a flicker of that old smile, but she could have imagined it.

"I've slept in worse places. Don't worry about me."

"Where will you put your things?"

Pete pointed toward a nearby coat closet. "It's not much, but I don't think Heath needs much room."

"You're correct," Heath said as he set Claire's bag and his laptop case on the recliner.

"Okay, then. I guess I'm ready for the tour." It seemed as if she was reminded of Heath's sacrifices every time she turned around, yet he hadn't complained once.

Pete followed her up the stairs to the loft. It wasn't even much of a bedroom. More like a bed in a room.

"The bathroom is downstairs, but you should have at least some privacy up here." Pete leaned over the railing as he spoke, clearly looking for Heath.

"Thanks. This is plenty of space."

Pete jerked his head toward the open room down from the loft. "You're in good hands. Heath is my friend, but I can say with confidence that he's also a skilled security agent."

"I know. He's been kind to me."

Pete looked around. "Well, this completes the tour."

Claire laughed, and the release felt amazing after hours of worry. "Thanks again."

Pete started down the stairs, and Claire followed. "I'm sure I'll be back. I can bring you some books if you'd like." When they reached the lower level, he pointed to a small shelf near the window that housed a dozen hardback action-adventure novels. "I'm not sure you'll be interested in those."

"I'd love a book or two."

"What are your preferences? I can get Jan at Stories and Scones to help me pick something they have in the store."

"I like classical literature, Shakespeare, and poetry. Oh, and I'd love a women's devotional. I forgot mine."

"Consider it done, Ms. Odom."

Heath stepped out of the hallway. "Everything looks great. Thanks again."

Pete slapped Heath on the back. "Anytime. I'll see you two soon. Give me a shout if you need anything."

After saying their good-byes to Pete, Heath

picked up her bag. "Would you like me to take this upstairs for you?"

"No, I can get it. I think I'd like to shower."

Heath pointed to a door in the hallway. "That's the only bathroom. I'll be in the living room setting up a remote office if you need anything. Adam should be here soon. He said he would bring dinner from Valentino's."

"Pizza delivery all the way out here?" Claire asked, clearly amused by the amenities provided at the safe house that she'd expected to be much more rustic and less accommodating.

"It was the only place I knew your order."

Oh, that made sense. He remembered her preference for pepperoni and black olives—the one they'd split the night they met.

"Valentino's sounds great. I'll get settled in and get that shower."

She grabbed everything she'd need to get clean. It was hard to believe they'd hiked for hours this afternoon. No wonder she was tired. That peaceful adventure at Freedom Lake felt like weeks ago.

Closing herself in the tiny bathroom, she avoided the mirror and got into the shower as fast as she could. It had been months since she'd thought of Jake by name, and she'd been forced to relive it all today. She'd trusted him—stupidly, of course. Her friend Tammy had sworn he was a good guy.

Now, Claire was locked away in a cabin with Heath, who she knew less than she'd known Jake when she'd agreed to that date and found out first-hand that he wasn't the stand-up guy her friends had claimed.

The walls seemed to be moving in on her, and the events of the last few days weighed heavy on her shoulders. Doubts mounted one on top of the other. She chanted a prayer as she scrubbed her hair and skin.

The Lord is with me. The Lord is with me.

She knew the words to be true, but her faith was slipping. How could the Lord leave her at a time like this? All the uncertainties were mounting, and her chest heaved in panic. The steamy air constricted in her chest.

Why couldn't she be normal? Did God really make her this way? Why did she break down at the first sign of trouble? Why couldn't she trust anyone she met?

She turned the lever to shut off the water and threw open the curtain. Her lungs screamed for air, but a steamy fog filled the hot room. She was stuck here with Heath, and he could overpower her in an instant. She'd never be able to protect herself.

After dressing in a rush, Claire burst out of the bathroom. The cool air crashed into her like a wave, and she filled her lungs in deep gasps.

Heath scrambled up from his seat on the couch. "Claire?"

She held up a hand, halting him in his tracks. "I need a minute."

He was across the room and in front of her in an instant. "Tell me what I can do to help?"

Her hand remained raised, stopping him a few feet away. He respected her request for space, and the ripping in her chest felt unwarranted. There had been plenty of chances for him to take advantage of her, but he hadn't given her the slightest inclination that she shouldn't trust him.

"I'm okay. I'm really okay. I had to talk about it today, and everything just came rushing back."

"What do you need? What can I do?"

Claire felt the pricking of tears behind her eyes. "Maybe one day I'll figure this out."

"It won't happen today. I know it feels urgent that you forget about what happened and get over it, but it's normal to have PTSD symptoms for years."

Of course. He'd served as a Marine, and for all she knew, he could have endured something that kept him up at night just like her. "I feel so stupid and weak. I hate it." Now the tears would come, whether she liked it or not. She linked her hands on top of her head and paced. If she could catch her breath, maybe she could calm down.

A rhythmic knock sounded, and they both looked to the door.

"That's Adam."

Claire took a deep breath, willing her heart to stop beating against her rib cage.

Heath jerked his head toward the couch. "You want to sit down? I'll get the stuff from him and be right back."

She plopped down on the seat and leaned forward, determined to get a handle on her panic before Adam left.

Heath disengaged the alarm on the high-tech control panel hidden by a sliding door near the entrance. "You get everything?"

"Everything. And Pete sent some books from Jan."

God bless that man. She knew she liked Pete.

"Good. I'll let you know if we need anything else. I logged into the network from here, so I'll be working Monday."

"Sounds good, Boss."

When she heard the door close, the garlic and tomato smell made its way into the room. She'd forgotten about the pizza.

She lifted her head when she heard Heath approaching. It was after eight at night, and he still wore his clothes from their hike, including his heavy boots.

He crouched in front of her and rested a hand on her arm. Worry was etched in lines on his forehead and between his brows. "Claire, what can I do to help?"

There was a peek of that kindness from earlier, and she let the words wrap around her heart. "I'm okay. I'm just processing." It was true, and she would probably be overthinking things and trying to come up with answers for a while.

"The pizza is here. You want me to bring it to you?"

A grin tugged at her mouth. A few sweet words from him sent all thoughts of the terrible day running away. She swiped at her cheek and straightened her shoulders. "I appreciate it, but I think it'll help if I get up and do something." He was being paid to keep her safe, not serve her dinner.

He rose to his feet and extended a hand to her. She took it and stood, relishing the anchor between them.

When he didn't pull away, she hesitated too.

Heath brushed a hand through his hair. "I know today has been chaotic and scary. I don't want you to think you're alone in this."

She'd been foolishly thinking he would use the opportunity being stuck in a cabin with her to take advantage of her. Shame clogged her throat. She stared at the floor. "I'm sorry. You've been so good to me."

Heath squeezed her hand, prompting her to look up. He studied her face with the determination of an artist. "I want to be here. With you. Don't ever doubt that."

She'd felt her heart open to him today at Freedom Lake, but that peaceful hike felt so far away. Since then, he'd closed himself off, only speaking to her to give instructions and prepare her for what would come next.

"I'm glad you're here," she whispered.

"I…" Heath rubbed a hand over his mouth.

Was he nervous?

"I wanted things to be different between us. I thought that after spending time with you today, you might want to go on a date with me."

Heat rushed to Claire's cheeks. He'd wanted to ask her on a date. The thought of dating before had always brought on crippling anxiety. There was none of that now.

"I would. I had a great time today."

Heath looked down at her hand in his. "But now things have changed. So fast. I need to be focused and alert. I have to be. I can't let anything happen to you."

Claire squeezed his hand and felt a grin tug the corners of her mouth. "You won't. I trust you."

Heath shook his head. "I would understand if you couldn't. Especially after what happened to you."

"A handful of therapists couldn't convince me of what you did today. I've been afraid of men and any kind of intimacy for years. I haven't trusted anyone. Until today. I trusted you, and I still do." She lifted their linked hands. "I haven't so much as bumped shoulders with a man since I left Savannah. This is a huge step for me."

"And I'm glad it was with me," Heath quickly added.

"Me too. I know you're not interested in that date anymore. There were a lot of things about me that you didn't know until this evening."

Heath shook his head again. "That's not it. I still want that for us, but I've never crossed that line with a client."

Realization left her cheeks tingling as the blood drained from her face. "Oh."

"With clients, I'm usually reserved. I don't speak unless necessary. I don't interfere unless I have to. It's my job to see and not be seen. I've tried to mentally prepare myself for that kind of interaction between you and me, but I don't think it's possible. I can't sit by while you're struggling with this. I want to be beside you, and I want to wrap you in my arms and dry your tears when you're crying."

Claire tugged her hand from his. "I understand. I—"

"What I'm trying to say is that I can't put up those walls with you like I do with everyone else. We started off differently, and I can't go back now. If you still want to, I'd like to take things slow. We can use this time together to get to know each other."

Of all the things she'd thought he was going to say, that wasn't anywhere close. "What about your job?"

"My co-workers know that we were together when this happened. I'll talk to them and see if they have any advice. They're good guys, and I trust them."

This was all surreal. Her emotions were swinging back and forth like a pendulum.

Heath brushed his thumb over the back of her hand. "I don't know what this means for us or where we'll end up, but I'd like to start with pizza."

Pizza. They had started with pizza forty-eight hours ago, and she couldn't think of a better way to break the ice.

She rested her forehead against his shoulder, and he hugged her tight. "I like pizza," she mumbled into his shirt.

His hand cradled the back of her head, and his soft whisper tickled her ear. "I like you."

12

HEATH

Sweat slid down Heath's neck and into the collar of his shirt. The dry, sandy heat burned his throat as it swirled into his lungs. He wiped his nose on his sleeve, leaving a streak of blood.

"That's your third nosebleed this week," Cameron joked. Why didn't he take his job seriously?

Heath watched the monitor, but the images and words were distorted. Was the building clear or not? Jackson hadn't given the signal. Was his radio out? Had he been captured?

"Just do it," Cameron said again.

"I can't. Not without a clear." Why didn't he just shut up?

Cameron scratched his arms, and Heath could

feel the tingling of sand mites through the thick sleeves of his uniform. Was he really itching? It was gone now.

Heath looked up, and the monitor in front of him faded away, revealing the beautiful lakeside spot where he'd stopped to eat lunch with Claire on their hike.

"This isn't Afghanistan." Heath looked around. "Claire?"

"That's the clear." It was Cameron again. What was he doing here?

Heath looked for the screen. He was back in Kandahar. The words were there, but the letters were backwards. He radioed in the clear and watched Knox's body cam as the team entered the building.

The explosion rocked the stone beneath Heath's feet all the way to the foundation. The shock waves pulsed through his body as debris rained from the ceiling.

This was the part where Heath screamed, but this time, he didn't. There was a blinding flash of white. When the scene cleared, Claire was standing by the lake.

No. She couldn't be here. This was the dream where everybody died, and it was all Heath's fault. Claire couldn't be a part of that.

The scream burst from his throat, and he sat

straight up. The sweat was real, but the smell of sand was replaced by the tinge of smoke in the air from the dying fire.

He clamped a hand over his mouth and willed his heartrate to slow. Pete's safe house was familiar, and it was all coming back to him now. Had he woken Claire? He listened hard, but there wasn't a rustling in the loft.

He threw off the blanket and put his feet on the floor. The nightmares were a regular reminder of the mistake he had to live with, but he hadn't dreamed of Kandahar in months. He rested his head in his hands. The flashback must be stress induced. He hadn't worried over an assignment in a long time, but his new situation with Claire had his nerves on edge.

The sun wasn't up yet, but he couldn't go back to sleep with his blood rushing through his veins as if he'd just completed a marathon. He checked his watch. It was 05:18. If Claire usually woke at six like she said, he could have breakfast ready for her. Making up his mind, he grabbed his boots and laced them. His buddy, Knox, had gotten caught before dawn without his shoes on at boot camp, and Heath had learned the lesson by association.

Knox. That familiar knife sheathed itself in Heath's gut. Any thoughts about his old friend only served to remind him that he couldn't make a mistake again.

He stoked the fire and added a log before quietly stepping into the kitchen and assessing the cabinets, pantry, and refrigerator. Everything was full. Pete had stocked this place in record time yesterday.

Remembering Pete's quick rundown of the cabin's security and safeguards, Heath eyed the pantry. He opened the door and grinned. A weapons stash behind the shelves of food was genius. He flipped a lever on the side wall and the shelving units pulled away revealing the hidden arsenal. Automatic rifles, pistols, batons, and knives sheathed in holsters lined the walls.

Heath made note of the inventory and closed the secret door. He'd have to thank his friend later.

Deciding on the morning menu, Heath fried the bacon first and used the grease for the eggs. The smell of meat and coffee mingled in the small kitchen, reminding him of the breakfasts his grandmother used to make on Christmas mornings when the whole extended family came over. His sisters hadn't cared about food when there were gifts to be ripped open, which left more for Heath. Real eggs were a treat after the powdered mush he'd had overseas. And he'd never eat spam for breakfast again after Honolulu. Bacon and eggs were two things that shouldn't be messed up.

He pulled two mugs from the cabinet when he heard Claire's quiet footsteps on the stairs. Right on time. "Good morning."

"How'd you know I was here?"

Heath looked over his shoulder and tried not to react when he saw her. Her straight hair was pulled back into a higher ponytail than he'd seen her wear. Her eyes opened lazily, but her smile was bright and cheerful.

"You're a heavy walker."

Claire gasped. "I am not."

Chuckling, he turned back to the coffee pot. "I'm joking. I've been listening for you."

"The amazing smell woke me. If I'd have known you were cooking, I'd have gotten my lazy bones up and helped."

"I don't mind. I just hope you like your eggs scrambled."

She smiled, and he felt a weird rumble in his middle. Since he wasn't hungry yet, it must be what some people call butterflies. Great. He was having involuntary reactions just because she was in the room. It had been less than twelve hours since he promised her they'd take things slow, but his central nervous system hadn't gotten the memo.

"I won't turn down an egg any way you cook it. Well, maybe not the super runny fried eggs. That just seems like a good way to get salmonella."

"Noted. Coffee? It's probably not as good as yours, but it'll wake you up."

"Yes, please." Claire picked up a piece of bacon and bit into it. "Oh wow. I'll gladly make the coffee if you keep cooking the bacon."

"It's a deal. I think everything is ready."

Heath poured a cup of coffee and stuck two slices of bread in the toaster while Claire filled her plate. When they sat with their food in front of them, Heath laid his hand on the table, palm up. "Mind if I say grace?"

She rested her warm hand in his. "Go ahead."

When the food was blessed, he released her hand. He had to let go now so they could eat, but would she want to hold his hand later? That was one way to take things slow—start with hand-holding. He shoved a forkful of eggs into his mouth to hide the grin that was spreading.

"What's so funny?" Claire asked.

Heath continued chewing as he pondered what to tell her. "You're cute, and I want to hold your hand" sounded lame, even in his head.

"Nothing is funny. I'm just not sure I should be enjoying this so much."

"Enjoying what?"

"Breakfast with you. It feels like a date or something, but you didn't actually agree to it."

Claire's eyes narrowed. "I can't say I've ever had a

breakfast date, but for the record, I would say yes to bacon and eggs with you any day."

Heath cleared his throat. This conversation could easily pass the "slow" speed he'd promised. "What are your plans for today?"

"I guess I need to paint, if I can."

"Why couldn't you? I thought Adam brought your supplies last night."

"He did, but there isn't a lot of room here." She looked over her shoulder at the common room that barely fit the couch he'd slept on. "I usually paint six canvases at a time, and I set them all up so I can go back and forth between them."

"We can make that work. I'll move some things around."

"I hate for you to have to do that. I think I have space for four as it is. Maybe three if we want to be able to walk around. And you need space to work too."

"I can work in the kitchen. We'll set up our spaces after breakfast. Tell me about what you're painting next."

Claire beamed with joy as she told him about her plans for the Freedom Lake series. She'd already chosen the colors, lighting, angles, and scenes. There was a definite method to her work.

When they'd finished eating, she cleaned their dishes while Heath started rearranging the furniture.

The couch and recliner were light and easy to push up against the wall. In two minutes, he had the whole room cleared like a dance floor.

Claire looked over the bar as she dried her hands on a towel. "Wow. That was fast."

"I'm thinking you could set up two on the bar and the other four in here."

"It's perfect." She propped her hands on her hips and studied the room. "Probably bigger than my studio at home."

"What else do you need?"

"Nothing. I'll let you have your space. I need to unpack my supplies, and I'll be all set."

"I'll be in the kitchen if you need me."

The kitchen table was tiny, but Heath didn't need much space. His remote office consisted of two laptops and a tablet. Pete's secure Wi-Fi was more than enough to keep Heath connected to everything he needed.

He sent an encrypted message to Jeremiah about the New Hope Gala and another to Adam letting him know to expect a supply list soon. Heath needed a few things from the office and his house.

He peeked over the top of his monitor and into the living room. Claire had changed into a paint-stained sweatshirt and loose-fitting jeans. She stood in front of one of the six easels she'd set up. Her attention pinged back and forth between the canvas and the paint she mixed on a pallet. A few stray hairs had escaped from her ponytail, framing her jawline.

Focus, Heath.

He had work to do, and that didn't include admiring his new client from across the cabin—the cabin that suddenly felt too small.

Email. He couldn't think about Claire if he was responding to emails.

Heath groaned as he opened his inbox. Thirty-six emails waited. He usually responded to messages as they came in or whenever he could spare twenty minutes throughout the day, but he'd spent the day with Claire yesterday and crashed when he was sure she was okay after her panic attack. Maybe Tessa had been right when she said he worked too much. Who got that many work emails on a Saturday?

The emails kept his attention until Claire stepped into the kitchen. She opened the pantry and stretched her arms over her head. Heath waited to see if she would notice the hinges for the hidden weapons stash, but she didn't.

So much for the email distraction. It was impossible to think about anything when Claire was so close.

She cleared her throat. "You want anything specific for lunch?"

Heath looked at the clock on his laptop. Had it

really been three hours? "Anything." At the mention of food, he felt the first pang of hunger.

Claire studied the contents on the shelves, then moved to the fridge. "Chicken and rice?"

"Sounds perfect. Let me help." He pushed out of his seat and began washing his hands.

"No, you go back to work. I need a break." Claire shooed him back toward his makeshift office.

"Are you sure? I can help."

"I'm really fine. It'll be ready in about an hour." She pulled the chicken from the fridge and put it in the sink before pulling a knife from the block on the counter.

"I'll make dinner," Heath offered.

"I won't say no to that."

Heath sat back at his computer and sent a message to Adam.

Heath: You get a rundown on Jake yet?

Adam: Just sent the preliminary to you.

Heath pulled up his email to find the investigative file for Jake Barnes waiting in his inbox. He scanned the report. It wasn't long. The criminal case court filings, Jake's sentencing, his parole reports, a list of addresses where he'd received mail in the last ten years, and a few photos. The investigator promised to follow up with current photos, a work history, and court transcriptions within forty-eight hours.

Heath's attention hung on the photos. They were from Hanover State Prison dated three years prior. He'd been imagining Claire's attacker to look rougher, but Jake Barnes looked more like a kid than a man. His sandy-blonde hair was tousled, and his expression was void of any emotion. His records claimed he weighed one hundred fifty-two pounds when he'd been incarcerated.

Jake could look like a completely different person now. He'd probably hit a growth spurt or two during those years in prison, and Heath tried to imagine what those changes might look like now.

"Heath?"

Heath jerked his attention from the photos.

Claire stood at the sink holding a head of lettuce. "Salad?"

The lifting of her brows told him this was the second time she'd asked the question. "Sure."

"I didn't mean to distract you from your work."

"It's okay. I'm used to Jeremiah and Adam walking into my office without knocking, so distractions don't bother me." Well, there was some truth to that. At headquarters, it was easy to answer a question and continue with his work. Here, Claire was an ever-present distraction that he didn't want to fight.

He looked back to the photo on the screen. "Actually, Adam just sent me a report on Jake Barnes."

Claire stiffened, slowly lowering the knife she held above the lettuce. "What?"

Heath rubbed the back of his neck. He was walking a fine line, but he'd never know how to address these things with her if he didn't find out now. "I messaged a private investigator yesterday evening about running a report on Jake Barnes. He's our best lead right now, so I wanted to see what he was up to and if we could find anything linking him to you. Recently."

Claire bit her lip and looked at the lettuce waiting to be washed and cored. "What does it say?"

"Do you want to see it? You don't have to if you don't want to."

There was a good chance the report would either be something she didn't want to face or cause her to panic, but he didn't feel right keeping it from her if she wanted to know. Seeing all the information might give her some closure.

She laid the knife down. "I think I do."

Heath stood and gestured that she should take his seat. Once she was settled in front of the screen, he leaned over her to click through different parts of the file.

"This is his prison report. He didn't have any infractions while he was locked up, and that granted him early parole."

Claire silently stared at the screen as Heath

flipped through different parts. Photos from Jake's social media accounts, school photos, transcripts, and traffic tickets.

"He didn't graduate either," Heath said.

Claire covered her mouth with one hand. "I know." She pointed to a photo, and Heath paused. "That. That's what he was wearing that night on our date."

"I wouldn't call it a date," Heath said, trying to keep the sneer from his tone.

"You're right about that. I had no idea what he was capable of when I met him at Johnny's Diner." Claire looked over her shoulder at Heath. "That's a little mom and pop place just outside the historic district. It was where our friends liked to hang out."

It sounded like any normal college date night. He'd gotten his degree in the military, and his college experience hadn't been anything like Claire's.

She pointed to the screen again. "This one is from that night. He must have met up with his friends before I got there."

Heath studied the image of Jake, smiling with his arm wrapped around a guy who sat in a booth beside him. Another guy hung over the back of the seat making a face and sticking bunny ears behind Jake's head.

"Do you know these other two?" Heath asked.

"I did. Garret and Dalton." She sighed. "They

were Jake's roommates, and they were called as witnesses at trial to testify that he hadn't been at their apartment at the time I claimed he attacked me."

Heath rested a hand on Claire's shoulder. "I wish I could take it all away." Heath could feel his jaw tensing and his teeth grinding together. "I hate that it happened to you."

She turned around and looked up at him. "I hate it too. I just wish I could get past it now. I went to counseling and group sessions for sexual abuse victims. So many people had it worse than me. I walked away with a few broken bones and bruises."

"That's nothing to downplay." Just the mention of her injuries made Heath's stomach turn.

"I know. It helped to talk about it and hear stories from other people. I felt like I couldn't talk about it to anyone in my life at the time. Who would understand? I liked going to those groups because it was a safe space, and I knew I wasn't alone and…"

"And what?"

"Broken. Damaged. Ruined. Some of the women were still learning to cope, but some of them were confident and powerful. I wanted that."

"You're not damaged or any of those things." Heath brushed the back of his fingers over her jaw. "You're strong, kind, talented, and smart. And you may be cautious when it comes to trusting new people, but that's warranted. You shouldn't trust everyone."

"I shouldn't have trusted him, but I trust you."

Those words hit Heath square in the chest, and he swallowed hard. He knew exactly what those words meant, and they pulled his heart to her a little more. "I won't let him hurt you again."

She smiled and whispered, "I know."

He wanted to kiss her. He'd never felt so drawn to a woman in his life, but kissing was too fast for Claire, and the last thing he wanted to do was accidentally trigger that fear in her again.

Claire broke their stare and cleared her throat. "I can't believe you got this much information in one night."

"My friend said he'd have more information within forty-eight hours."

"So soon?"

"He's flying out to Gainesville, Florida tonight. That's where Jake lives now."

Claire's eyes widened. "He's going to actually watch him?"

"Just for a few days. We want to see if he is associated with anyone else we might want to look into."

"You said this is a friend of yours? The one doing the investigating?"

"Yes. I've known him for years, and I trust him."

Claire looked back at the photos. "You sure have a lot of friends."

Heath had met hundreds of people during his time with the Marines, and he'd consider many of them friends. He could think of no less than two dozen men he could call today who would drop everything to help him if he asked. "I guess I do. I've worked with a lot of people over the years, and many of them became friends." Heath felt a sharp tearing in his chest. Claire didn't seem to have that support network. "Claire?"

She looked up at him as if pulled from a daze.

"Do you have friends? People you can count on if you need something?"

She shrugged. "Just Tessa. And my parents. I had friends in college, but I wasn't a good friend after the incident."

"Why not?"

"I wasn't happy. I wasn't any fun to be around."

Heath crouched beside her chair. He didn't like standing over her while they had this talk. "It's not a true friendship if you have to be entertaining to be accepted."

"I know. I have Tessa now. She showed me that."

"She's a good one, and good luck getting rid of her. She hangs on like a dog with a bone."

Claire chuckled and wiped her eyes. Heath hadn't

seen any tears, but she was probably having a hard time taking in all the information about Jake.

"Thank you." She stood and wiped her hands down her shirt. "I should get the salad ready. You did say you wanted salad, right?"

Heath stood, giving her space to move around him in the small kitchen. "Sounds great. I was thinking we should call Tessa later. I know she's worried about you."

Claire smiled. Seeing happiness on her face was like breaking the surface of the water after being under too long. He needed to see her smile. It felt as vital as filling his lungs with air.

She nodded. "I'd like that."

13

CLAIRE

Claire pushed her plate toward the center of the table. "I can't eat another bite."

Heath rested back in his chair with a cocky grin. "I told you."

"You told me you made good spaghetti. You did not tell me the dangers of overindulging." She rubbed a hand over her stomach, which felt uneasy and full of the delicious pasta and meat sauce.

"Maybe we can take a hike one day soon. I feel like I need to run a few miles to work off the carbs."

Claire sat forward in her excitement. "Could we?"

"I think it would be okay. I could get Derek to scout the area with one of his dogs in the morning. I wouldn't want to go far though. We're already a long way from help if we needed it."

She held up her wrist. "I have the bracelet. Does it work even when I'm not at my house?"

"It does. And I guess I should show you how to call for help if you need it."

Claire's back straightened. "But you'll be here."

"I will. But it's always best if you know these things in case the worst happens." He stood and grabbed both of their dishes.

"Okay. But I don't like that kind of thinking." She was here for protection in case the worst happened. She didn't like imagining the millions of possibilities that could be, much less facing it without Heath.

"This place has many protections already in place. Think of it as your backup bodyguard."

Claire straightened her shoulders. "Okay, what do I do?"

Heath dried his hands after rinsing the dishes and opened the pantry. He pointed to the inside wall. "See this?"

Claire peered inside and saw a metal switch. "Yeah."

He flipped it, and the shelves of the pantry swung out to reveal a full-sized opening. Guns and other things she didn't recognize lined the walls.

"Whoa. You weren't kidding about the backup bodyguard. Please tell me this house knows how to use these things, because I don't."

Heath laughed. "It's very unlikely we'd need to

use a weapon. The perimeter alarm will let us know someone is coming with enough time to get out."

"Get out?"

Heath extended his hand, and she took it, following him as he ducked into the narrow passageway. Dim lights illuminated the hall, and her attention darted from Heath to the floor and back.

He led her a few feet into the corridor to a dark door. "This leads outside." He tapped a small keypad, and it lit up. "The code is 091847."

"Oh, that's easy to remember. A bunch of random numbers I'll have to recall in an emergency."

Heath chuckled and squeezed her hand. "It's the date the CIA was founded. Pete is a former secret agent."

"What? The insurance guy? I wondered why he had a place like this."

"Pete is a man of many secrets. Most of them he'll have to take to his grave."

"Wow. What a life."

Heath tugged her hand. "There's more." He pointed to a narrow stairway leading up.

"No wonder the cabin is so small, half of it is hidden away." She looked left and right, but nothing was discernable. "Where does this lead?"

Heath rested his hand on a wall that blocked the top of the stairway. "You use the same code here." He entered the numbers and the door swung open.

Claire peeked around Heath's shoulder and gasped. "It's the loft."

"If anyone tries to break in while you're upstairs, try to get to this entrance. It's behind the bookshelf." Heath showed her how it closed, leaving a nondescript piece of furniture hiding the door to the secret exit. "Close it behind you, and it'll lock. You'll be able to get out the door downstairs with the code. There's a small drop-off about thirty yards from this exit. If you can get to it, there's a ledge about six feet down. There's a slight indention in the hill where you can hide."

"What if I can't find it?"

Heath stepped closer to her, strengthening her with his presence. "I'll show you tomorrow. Hopefully, you won't need to know any of this. We're just preparing for the worst."

"Right. I feel a little better knowing all this."

Heath pointed to a brown throw blanket on the foot of the bed. "If you think about it, bring a blanket with you. You can drag it behind you to hide your footprints in the snow and use it to stay warm while you hide out."

"What if I—?"

Heath stopped her with a hand on each of her shoulders. "If you don't bring it, shuffle your feet as you walk. You've got this. Most importantly, you have me, and I'll guide you through all of this if we ever need to get out fast."

Claire nodded. "Okay. I know that." She felt the twinge in her nose and the pricking behind her eyes that told her tears weren't far. Why was she crying again? She hated crying, and she wanted Heath to see her being brave, not a blubbering mess.

Heath put his warm arms around her shoulders, and she sank into his embrace, wrapping her own arms around his sides and up his back.

Her tears fell silently before soaking into his shirt. How did she end up here? She'd always been a rule follower. She'd always tried to do good to others. She went to church. She studied for tests. She was never late. Why her?

Heath's words rumbled against her cheek that rested on his chest. "I know you're scared. I know you're tired of being on guard and worrying." He paused, rubbing a rhythmic circle on her back. "But have you prayed about this?"

"Of course," she whispered. "I pray all the time."

"You might not be praying for the right thing."

She raised her head. "What do you mean?"

"God made you with a special intention for your life. We don't always know what our purpose will be until it's here. Sometimes, we have to put ourselves aside—deny ourselves—before we can see the path God has in store for us."

"I'm not sure I have a purpose. What could it possibly be?" she asked in disbelief.

"I don't know that. You have to let your faith be bigger than your fear."

Claire froze and stared at him. She'd always assumed her faith was strong. She'd never doubted her belief in the Lord, but Heath was right. She'd been so adamant that she should be able to over-come her own fear that she hadn't thought to step aside to make way for God to do His work through her.

"I've never thought of it that way."

"We all have doubts and fears, but sometimes we don't get the answers we're looking for until we lay the things we can't control at His feet."

Claire stared at Heath as if seeing him for the first time. She'd been to countless counselors and group therapies, and nothing she'd heard in any of those meetings had resonated the way Heath's words did now.

He took a step back, assessing her face. "I know it's easier said than done, but—"

"You're right," she interrupted. "That's something I need to do." With a somewhat clear course of action, she felt a thrumming in her chest that begged her to get to work now.

"If there's anything I can do to help you, please tell me."

"Really, you've done so much. You're helping me all the time."

She held his gaze as she looked up at him. The intensity in his eyes sent a fire over her skin, and she didn't know what came next. Would he kiss her?

His gaze lowered to her mouth before quickly returning to her eyes. He leaned in slowly, and her heart beat wildly in her chest.

This would be her first kiss since she was attacked. It was four years ago, but it felt like an eternity. Did she even know how to kiss? Could she forget something like that? There had been so few even before the incident in college.

Instead of kissing her, Heath pressed his forehead to hers. She closed her eyes, breathing in the assurance of his presence. This was what a relationship was supposed to be—two people who trusted each other.

She hadn't been sure if she was ready for Heath to kiss her or not until now. Knowing that he could have, wanted to, and chose not to because he'd promised to take things slow for her sake meant he was worthy of all her trust.

Romance wasn't kissing and roses. It was trust and faith wrapped up in the most beautiful bow.

Their noses brushed against each other, and her smile widened.

"What's got you smiling?" Heath whispered.

She couldn't say "This is the most intimate moment I've ever experienced," so she went for something tamer but also truthful.

"You smell good."

Heath laughed and lifted his head. "Good to know."

"Do you wear cologne?" It didn't smell like a chemical from a bottle, but it was masculine and fresh.

Why was she overanalyzing his scent?

"Thistle and black pepper bodywash. My sister got it for me for my birthday."

"That's so sweet. Speaking of your sister, we should call Tessa."

"Let me secure the line." He reached for her hand and led her down the narrow staircase. Thankfully, they didn't have to go down the way they'd come up through the secret passageway.

Heath found his phone in the kitchen, a new one he'd gotten from Got Your Six headquarters before they left. Had that only been yesterday? She felt as if she'd aged ten years since then.

He dialed the number and handed it to Claire. "It's all yours."

She heard Tessa's voice as soon as she put the phone to her ear.

"What's happening? Where are you?"

"Calm down. Everything is fine."

Tessa huffed. "Who are you, and what have you done with my friend?"

Claire laughed. "I know. That's usually your line."

"Now stop joking around. Are you okay? I called you yesterday to see how your hike with Heath went, and you didn't answer—any of the fifteen times I tried. So I called your mom, and she said you were still with Heath. It was ten at night! She said something happened, and you were hiding out. She wouldn't even tell me where!"

"I'm so sorry I didn't get in touch with you sooner. When Heath and I got back to my house after the hike, someone shot at us."

"What?" Tessa yelled.

Claire pulled the phone from her ear.

"Let me talk to Heath!" Tessa said just as loudly as her last comment.

Claire passed the phone to Heath, who put it on speakerphone and laid it on the table.

"Hello."

"Heath Bradley Mitchell, you better tell me why someone is shooting at you and Claire. Right now."

Heath grinned a little at his sister's dramatics. "We're not sure yet, but we're working on a lead."

"I need updates. As soon as you get them."

Heath looked up at Claire and raised a brow.

"You can tell her," Claire said.

"I'll keep you posted," Heath promised.

"I need to lie down or something. Is this what the vapors feels like? I may faint."

Claire leaned down closer to the phone on the table. "Don't worry. Heath is here. You said yourself he's the best at what he does."

Tessa's end of the line was silent for a moment. "I did say that. He is."

"Okay, then take a breath," Claire said.

A whoosh sounded on Tessa's end of the line. "Okay. You're right. Heath, you got this?"

"I got this," Heath promised.

"Good. Keep my friend safe. She's special."

Claire looked to Heath, and his warm gaze was fixed on her.

"I know." The assurance in his voice made Claire's chest swell with happiness.

"So where are you?" Tessa asked.

"We can't tell you that," Heath said quickly.

"We're safe," Claire said. "I'm with Heath, and we're safe."

"I guess that's all I need to know." Tessa sighed. "Call me soon?"

"We will," Claire promised. "Love you, Tess."

"Love you. Both of you."

"Take care. Love you too," Heath said.

Heath disconnected the call, and they stood silently for a moment. They didn't know when it would be safe to talk freely with their friends again, but Claire was glad to have Heath beside her until this was over.

14

HEATH

*H*eath stood from the hard wooden chair at the kitchen table. His makeshift desk was uncomfortable, but he'd made do with worse. "Can I see yet?"

She'd been hiding the unfinished pieces, claiming they weren't fit to be seen yet. He remembered her explanation from a few days ago when she'd said that looking at a painting before it's finished is like taking a bowl of flour and eggs and expecting it to look like a cake.

Claire peeked her head out from behind a canvas that rested on an easel in the living room. "Almost. I'll finish it after supper."

No wonder his back ached. It was five in the afternoon. Time seemed to either creep or fly in this cabin. Some days, work kept him busy from dawn to dusk. Other days, he fought boredom and pestered Claire to let him see her paintings.

The perimeter alarm sounded, and Claire jerked her wide eyes to Heath.

He raised his hands. "Don't worry. It's Pete. He told me he was coming."

Claire's shoulders sagged in relief. She'd been surprisingly relaxed this week, and they were both thankful it had been an uneventful stay at Pete's secret cabin so far. He didn't want her getting spooked by the alarm.

She put her paintbrush in a cup of water and stretched her arms. "I can't wait to see what he had Jan pick out for me this time. It's kind of nice having a personal book shopper."

"Jan is perfect for that job. Have you met her?"

"Not that I know of."

"I'll have to introduce you soon." Hopefully, he could make that happen sooner rather than later.

Heath met Pete at the door and accepted the grocery bags and boxes. "Hey, man. Good to see you."

"You as well." Pete looked around the small cabin and smiled when he spotted Claire. "Jan sent some good things for you."

"I can't wait to thank her," Claire said. "And thank you for all this."

Pete rubbed the back of his head. "Is there any

way you could not mention that you're hiding out at my safe house when you meet Jan? She doesn't know about this part of my life." He waved his hands around, indicating the technologically advanced cabin.

Claire raised her hands in surrender. "Sure. That's none of my business."

"I told her you were staying at one of my properties, which is true. She sent some of her scones this time too." Pete put a hand up beside his mouth and pretended to share a secret. "The orange are my favorites."

Claire craned her neck to see the bags Pete had brought in. "I won't say no to that."

"What about me?" Heath said.

Pete bumped his friend's shoulder. "You can have whichever one Claire doesn't like."

"I see how it is."

"I wish I could stay, but I have to stop by another property on my way back. Call me if you need anything else."

"We appreciate it."

"Bye," Claire said with a cheery wave.

Heath closed the door and locked it before he pointed to the bags. "Let's see what we can put together for dinner tonight."

"It's my turn to cook. Any suggestions?"

Heath peered into a bag and quickly closed it.

"Actually, I want to cook tonight. You finish that painting."

Claire laughed. "You really want to see it?"

"Of course I do. You'll have about an hour before the food is ready."

She turned on her heel and settled herself in front of the painting. Heath pulled the steaks from the bag and put them in marinade. He loved grilled ribeye, but he'd settle for pan seared. Hopefully, Claire would enjoy the treat. He'd have to thank Pete later.

He got to work preparing dinner and snuck glances at Claire from time to time. The anticipation of seeing her painting was the highlight of his week. He wanted to see what she'd created. He needed to see if her depiction of Freedom Lake matched his own. It felt like a special part of Claire that he wanted to know.

He pulled salad and baked potato toppings from the fridge, looking for anything and everything that Claire might like.

Slowly yet all at once, his days had turned into a blissful domestic existence with a woman he was falling for, and the realization scared him and thrilled him at the same time. What would it be like to go back to his regular routine? He would miss Claire and her sweet good mornings. He would miss their shared meals and the fun conversations they had as they got to know each other.

They were playing house, and things were going too well. This wasn't real life, but it looked like a snapshot of what he wanted. A simple life with a woman who loved him.

Love? Could they have that? He'd promised to take things slow, but his feelings for Claire were quickly speeding past the yield sign.

"Finished."

Heath dropped the butter and shredded cheese on the counter and sprinted for the living room. "I can see it?"

"You can see it." Claire stepped aside and gestured to the canvas.

He wasn't sure what he'd expected, but the painting was much better than the real Freedom Lake. The colors were bold and beautiful, blending seamlessly with shadows that made the painting seem more real than its two dimensions.

"Whoa. That's amazing."

Claire chuckled. "Can I quote you on my website?"

"Feel free because I have no other words."

"This has been my favorite series. Thank you for taking me there."

Heath ripped his attention from the painting to

look at Claire. She was thanking him, but he felt like the blessed one. "I don't want to take anything away from your dad, but I'd love to see other places with you."

She looked up at him with a sparkle in her eyes. "I'd love that."

Love must be in the air because his attention caught on the word every time he heard it, and he had no intention of steering away from it when Claire was beside him.

The microwave beeped, startling him from the trance he'd been locked in. Claire had a way of captivating his full attention.

"Dinner is almost ready."

"Good." Claire wiped her hands on a rag. "I'll wash up and meet you in the kitchen."

Minutes later, the steaks were hot off the stove and the salad toppings were spread all over the counter.

Claire inhaled a deep breath. "It smells amazing. Is that steak?"

"I hope you like your meat rare."

Claire's eyes widened. "Well, I—"

Heath laughed. "I'm joking. I actually cooked a few different temperatures. I'll eat whatever you don't eat."

"You're spoiling me, Mr. Mitchell."

Heath rested his back against the counter at her side and gave her a playful wink. "I aim to please."

She turned away as a blush crept up her cheeks. "Stop it."

"Stop what?"

"Being too sweet for your own good. You're impossible to resist as it is."

Heath pushed off the counter and straightened. "Really?"

"As if you didn't know," Claire huffed, but her smile betrayed her joy.

"Let's eat. I'm starving."

"Don't rush me. I'm taking my time with this feast."

They talked and laughed as they ate. It would be difficult to leave this life when the real world crashed the party. Funny, he'd never thought of work as a party before. He'd definitely stepped outside the boundaries he'd set for Got Your Six Security during this time with Claire. Jeremiah had voiced his opinion that the relationship was fine as long as Heath's focus wasn't compromised.

Focus was one thing he didn't worry about. He'd been working day and night with the investigator.

Claire rested her fork and knife on the plate. "I can't eat another bite."

"Me either. I wanted to wait until after dinner to tell you, but the investigator sent more info on Jake."

Claire straightened her back. "Really? What was it?"

Heath stood with both of their plates. "Let's talk about it in the living room."

They cleared the dishes and cleaned up the dinner mess in record time. Heath grabbed his laptop and settled next to Claire on the couch. They'd formed a routine after dinner where they read and talked on the couch until bedtime when they went their separate ways.

Opening the file, Heath scrolled to the last report. "He works at a Walmart distribution warehouse in Gainesville. He doesn't have any active social media accounts." He pulled up the latest photos. "These are from this week."

The first photos showed Jake walking into the warehouse. His T-shirt sported the company logo, and he'd gained a good twenty pounds since the last photos.

"He looks different," Claire said.

"My friend said he visited a counseling clinic on Tuesday. He was with a woman on Monday night, and he attended church on Wednesday evening."

"Church? That's good, right?" she asked.

"We can only hope. It doesn't make sense. My friend says he's been a model citizen. I know that looks and behavior can sometimes be deceiving, so we'll continue to keep an eye on him."

Claire rested back against the couch. "Wow. I can't believe I'm not freaking out about this. Actually, hearing all this makes me calmer. It's almost like knowing more is helping me process it."

"Good. I'll try not to bring it up unless there's something else you need to know."

"You're really good at what you do. I'm glad we met. I'd be falling apart right now without you."

"I'm glad we met too."

"It seems like perfect timing." She smoothed her hair back and leaned on his shoulder. "What's it like being a bodyguard?"

"There's not a lot of action involved if you can believe it. Most of the work is done behind the scenes."

"Like the surveillance cameras and stuff?"

"Exactly. We don't use weapons unless it's absolutely necessary, but we train with them just in case."

"What was it like with the Marines?"

"A different world. It was challenging and awesome. I loved it."

"Why'd you leave then?"

Suddenly, his jaw tightened, and the breath he'd been inhaling clogged his throat. "I didn't want to."

Claire raised her head and looked up at him. "I'm sorry."

She wanted an explanation, but he didn't know how to tell her. He'd messed up and killed two of his brothers—men he'd devoted his life to protecting. She'd question how he could protect her if he couldn't protect those he'd been charged to lead. If he told her the truth, he'd lose all the faith and trust he'd gained.

Fake. He was a fake. He hadn't been good enough to do his job then. What made him think he was good enough now? He wasn't good enough for Claire either. He'd called Adam no less than a dozen times this week to ask for a second set of eyes on the surveillance Heath had already checked. There was too much at stake, and another mess-up would mean more lives lost.

Claire's life lost.

She rested her soft hand over his. The warmth of her touch did little to dispel the nagging shame.

"You don't have to talk about it," she whispered.

Even if he didn't talk about it, nothing would change. The deaths had been an accident, but that blood was still on his hands.

"I'm sorry." The words were out before he knew what he was saying. Of course he was sorry. He hadn't read the signal correctly and sent men into a building to their deaths. He was sorry for their families and friends. He was sorry for failing his brothers. He hadn't wanted to leave because he'd loved his job, but he couldn't go on with his days with the weight of that mistake hanging over him. He didn't deserve the position or any advancements or achievements.

He should have saved lives, not lost them.

"Heath."

Claire raised her hand to his face and brushed the tips of her fingers over his cheek. "Don't go there. Stay here, with me."

He shouldn't go there—in his thoughts or in his dreams—but that didn't stop it from happening.

But he wasn't there. He was here with Claire, and it may be wrong to want this happiness, but he couldn't fight the pull he felt toward her.

Her expression was soft and comforting as her gaze followed the trail of her fingers over his jaw and down his neck. The slow tickle over his skin sent a lick of heat up his spine.

In a world full of bad, she was the good. And he wanted every bit of this.

His chest swelled as her fingers fell over the collar of his shirt and moved down. Her open palm rested warm and steady over his heart.

"You can tell me anything, but you don't have to. You've been so patient with me, and I want to be that for you."

Heath swallowed hard. Claire Odom was a combination of everything he hadn't known he wanted in a woman. She was a perfect mix of kindness, determination, faithfulness, and understanding. He couldn't deny that she'd worked her way into his heart starting the moment he met her.

The urge to lean in and seal his lips with hers was strong, but he fought it. This wasn't about him. It was about her, and he'd agreed to let her set the pace of their relationship. The waiting would be worth the reward. Claire would always know she could trust him to put her needs above his own.

He rested his hand atop hers on his chest. "You're doing everything right. It's just a hard time to talk about, and I really don't know what to say yet."

She nodded, and her grin pulled a little wider. "Okay."

Her gaze dropped to his mouth. Did she want him to kiss her?

Heath slowly slid his hand up her arm and over her shoulder, watching her expression for any sign of alarm.

"Is this okay?" he asked.

"Yes." Her word was quiet but steady in her assurance.

He brushed his hand up her neck and gently cradled the side of her head. "And this?"

"Yes."

"Can I kiss you?" He said the words so softly they were barely audible.

"Yes."

With her permission, he slowly brushed his lips over hers. She moved with him, dancing her mouth over his. A burst of energy ignited in all the places they touched and pulsed throughout his body in a steady, controlled flood that filled him to the brim.

She fisted her hand on his chest, gripping his shirt as he fought the urge to pull her in for more.

Slow. This *was* slow. Their movements were slow, but their hearts were racing. Slowly kissing Claire did nothing to temper the wildfire inside him, all-consuming and unstoppable.

An alarm sounded, jolting them apart.

Claire's eyes were wide. "The perimeter alarm."

Heath raced to the kitchen and pulled up the surveillance feed on his laptop. His heart raced even as he realized the cause for alarm. "It's a bear."

Claire was beside him, leaning over his shoulder in an instant. Between the rush of the kiss and the adrenaline surge of the alarm, his heart rate might never calm down.

Claire rested a hand on her chest. "Thank goodness."

Heath brushed a hand through his hair. Saved by the bear. As much as he'd wanted to keep kissing Claire, he knew it was best to give her some space. He said slow, and he intended to keep his word. The thought of damaging that fragile trust terrified him as much as the unknown danger they faced.

Her arms wrapped around him. "This is all so scary, but I feel safe when you're here."

He turned in the chair and embraced her middle.

A pang of guilt ripped through his chest. For all her faith in him, he wasn't the man she thought he was. He wanted to keep her safe more than anything, and his conscience warred with reason. He was falling for her, and he was easily distracted every time she was near.

They had one shot with no room for error. Swallowing hard, he held her tighter and said a prayer. He had no leads and no suspects, which meant Claire's safety was still at stake.

"I need to do some more work. I'll catch up with you in a little while."

Claire's arms loosened around him. "Okay, let me know if you need anything."

Her lips brushed over his forehead, and she ascended the stairs to the loft. Alone in the kitchen, he cradled his head in his hands and prayed for guidance and wisdom.

15

CLAIRE

*T*he mid-December wind stole the breath from Claire's lungs as she trudged through the snow at Heath's side. Her nose was numb and tingling, and the cold was seeping through her boots to her toes.

She panted for each breath that produced one word. "Remind me again why I wanted to do this."

Heath stomped his snow-covered boots on the porch of the safe house. "We're back now. You start the coffee, and I'll tend the fire."

The warmth of the cabin wrapped around her like a blanket as she stepped inside. "I did want to walk the path again. I'm afraid I'll get lost if I have to do it alone."

Three weeks ago, the thought of running from a faceless enemy into the vast Rocky Mountains would have terrified her. Heath had gone over so many escape routes and backup plans that she felt about eighty-five percent confident that she wouldn't die of hypothermia if she had to venture out alone.

"It's a real long shot that you would ever have to leave this cabin without me. Please don't worry."

The familiar fear didn't come, and warmth filled her chest. She'd finally begun healing those broken and scarred places in her heart thanks to Heath. He put her on the right track.

Actually, she needed to thank Jan too. She'd sent a sweet devotional in her last book bundle that paired perfectly with Heath's advice. Her faith was now greater than her fear, and there was a sense of freedom in knowing she didn't need to save herself. God had a plan for her, and she was brave enough to face it with Him at her side.

She'd just poured the first scoop of coffee into the maker when Heath's satellite phone rang. Her shoulders remained relaxed, and she gave herself a mental pat on the back. Every sound had sent her into a panic when she'd first come to the safe house.

She could only hear Heath's half of the short conversation, and his last sentence drew her attention.

"I'll tell her."

It could be anyone. Surely, he had other female

clients. He'd told her a little bit about the types of protection he offered to companies and at events. It seemed less exciting than she'd imagined.

"That was Adam. He said your mom called the office today and asked him to get a message to you. They haven't heard from you in a few days and want to talk."

"Did it sound urgent?"

"No. I think they just like hearing from you that you're safe."

"Is it safe to call them?"

"I think so. We secure the line each time."

The coffee was brewing, and she had half an hour before she needed to start making lunch. "Can I call them now?"

"Sure. Let me secure the line."

He handed her the phone, and she rested back on the couch. Going outside for even a short time zapped her energy. It was too cold to do anything except shiver.

"Hello." Her mother's eager greeting relaxed her even more.

"Hey. Is Dad with you?"

"Yes. Let me get him." Her mother whispered, "Danny, get over here. It's Claire."

"How are you, baby?" Her mom didn't wait for her dad to join before bounding into the conversation.

"I'm fine. Heath doesn't have any new leads, and he's been teaching me how to be safe and think ahead in case something happens."

"My heart can't take much more of this," her mother said.

"Claire Bear?" her dad asked.

"Hey, Dad. Everything is fine here."

"I've been so worried."

"You don't have to be," Claire assured. "Heath is taking good care of me." She wasn't sure exactly when her fear had subsided, but it was completely gone now.

"Good. He seems like a nice guy," her dad said. "Are you sure you're okay staying there with him? There isn't any funny business going on, is there?"

"Dad! There is *no* funny business happening here." Her cheeks flooded with warmth. Her parents knew her well enough to know she wasn't purposefully shacking up with a stranger and fooling around. And they knew enough about her aversion to dating to know she'd speak up in a heartbeat if she wasn't comfortable around Heath.

"I believe you. He seems like a good guy. My friend Pete said good things about Heath."

"You know Pete O'Rourke?"

"We went to school together. When he heard about what happened, he called to check on you and let us know he's praying for your safety."

"And our sanity," her mother added.

"How sweet of him."

"He said Heath is the best in the biz," her dad said.

Claire peeked into the kitchen where Heath sat at his makeshift desk, engrossed in his work once again. Of course he was the best in the biz. He took his job seriously.

"He is. I don't think there are any new leads. If you think I should terminate his services and go home, I'm okay with that." Her parents had been helping her pay the Got Your Six Security fees, which seemed minimal compared to what she'd expected. He'd probably given her a discount.

"Oh no," her mother protested. "We want Heath to stay with you as long as it takes. Really, sweetie, we can afford it, and your safety is worth it."

"He's really great. I don't feel as scared and helpless. I do think I need to confess that I like him. I promise, there's really no funny business. He knows about Savannah, and we're just taking things slow and getting to know each other."

"Are you sure you know what you're doing?" her dad asked.

Claire's chuckle was awkward and forced. "Of course I don't. I have no idea how to have a boyfriend."

"But you'll learn," her mom promised. "Heath

may or may not be the one for you, but I think it's wonderful that he's patient enough to give you time to work through your insecurities."

"Thanks. I love you both."

"We love you too, sweetie," her mom said.

"Call us when you can," her dad said. "We like to hear that you're okay."

"Love you too." The call ended, and she rested back on the couch with her eyes closed.

"You want to make gingerbread cookies?" Heath asked.

Heath was standing at the end of the couch holding a box of cookie mix. "We don't have a cookie cutter, but it says we can make drop cookies if we don't have a cutter. I have no idea what that means."

Claire tried to conceal her laugh. "It's just regular round cookies."

"Oh, good. You like gingerbread? It's all Pete sent this time, but we can get another next time."

She pushed off the couch and walked straight into Heath's arms. "Gingerbread is perfect. I've been missing the signs of Christmas around here."

"I imagine that's why Pete sent them. I hate that you're not getting to enjoy the Christmas fun around town."

Claire rested her head on his chest, soaking in the soothing rhythm of his heartbeat. "I'm actually more in the Christmas spirit this year than I normally am. I've had a lot of uninterrupted time to study the Word, and Jan has sent some great devotionals. My mind has been clearer here, and I focus better."

"That's good. I'm sorry you haven't gotten to go to church the last few weeks."

"I miss it," she admitted.

"Me too."

"I feel like I've had a reset these last few weeks. It's like I've been shown what's important in my life."

Heath hugged her tighter. "Me too." He rested his forehead against hers and took a deep breath. "I don't want to rush you or scare you off, but I'm falling for you. I know it hasn't been a long time, but I know how I feel about you. There's no question. I've never felt anything even close to this before. I still think we should take things slow, but I want you to know where I stand. I'm not going anywhere."

How had she stumbled into this wild and crazy ride with Heath? He was the perfect man to help her grow in courage and faith.

"I'm falling for you too. I don't know how we got here, but I'm not scared of what comes next for us."

Heath's warm brown eyes stared back at her. "You're amazing."

"You showed me how to be brave."

Heath brushed his fingertips over her jaw,

igniting every nerve-ending in her body. "I'm just the armor. You're the warrior."

She'd been searching for trust, support, and understanding, and she'd found all of that and more in Heath Mitchell. He built her up and cheered her on, assuring her that she was better and stronger than she believed.

She loved him, and there was no going back now.

16

HEATH

*T*he transformation in Claire was huge. She wasn't looking over her shoulder anymore, and Heath had to hope it was because she trusted him.

Speaking of that trust, he needed a lead on whoever was after her. Got Your Six and the local PD had run into a wall. Jake Barnes hadn't taken a suspicious step in weeks, and they'd been following him closely enough to know. He went to work, hung out at a woman's house, and attended church whenever the doors were open.

It didn't make sense, but there hadn't been so much as a scrap of evidence left from the sidewalk incident or the shooting at her house. Tire tracks and a dead-end trail in the woods weren't much to go on.

Claire closed the oven door and tossed the baking gloves onto the counter. "I'm setting a timer and taking a shower. Will you check on them in a little bit? If they look dark around the edges, take them out early."

"I can do that."

"Is baking something they teach Marines?" A playful smile danced on her lips.

"Not at all. Cora is the baker in the family. I have to say this is my first attempt."

"You'll do fine." Claire's eyes fell closed as she soaked up the sugar and spice in the air. "It definitely smells like Christmas in here."

"Sorry I couldn't get you any decorations."

Claire tilted her chin up for a kiss, and Heath's arms wrapped around her without a second thought. When her lips brushed against his, every thought in his head vanished. These moments with her had become too commonplace, and as much as he wanted more of her adoring kisses, they needed to pump the brakes and put some space between them. Playing house with Claire was too easy.

Breaking the kiss, he rested his forehead against hers. "I'm going to get you out of here."

"I know you will." She rested her hands on his chest and thrummed her fingertips against the thick material of his hoodie. "I'm glad we have this time to get to know each other, but I don't like the idea of living with my boyfriend."

He covered her hands with his. "I know. This isn't how I wanted to start things with you either. We'll get to have a normal relationship soon." He lifted her hand and kissed it. "Until then, you still have my word that we won't cross any lines."

Her lips met his in a quick and sure kiss before she took a step back. "I should be back before the cookies are done."

Heath sat back at his computer with renewed determination. Notifications and messages waited, and he scanned each of them, noting which had already been taken care of by Adam or Jeremiah.

The surveillance camera on Heath's doorbell sent a video message each time movement was detected in front of his house. The latest video clip showed a mail carrier dropping off a package near the front door.

He sent a message to Tessa asking her to pick it up. It was the new tactical gloves he'd ordered for the guys at work.

The video clip reached the end and began replaying. A black sedan parked on the street caught his eye. A memory of the car coming toward him on the sidewalk caused him to pause. It couldn't be the same vehicle. Could it?

His blood pressure rose as he flipped through

other clips. The vehicle was there every time a package had been delivered to his door.

If anyone knew about the car, it was Bob. The old neighbor knew everything that went on in their neighborhood. Heath dialed the number and secured the line. His surety grew with each pounding heart-beat, and he prayed Bob had an explanation.

After five rings, the old man answered with a friendly, "Ello."

"Hey, Bob. What's the story on that black car in front of your place?"

"You on vacation?"

Bob hadn't picked up on Heath's urgency. "Yes. Is the car yours?"

"No. It's been there for weeks. I was thinkin' about reportin' it."

"Does it ever leave? Is anyone in it?"

"It leaves for a while and comes back. I seen a man in it once. I couldn't tell from my window, so I went for a walk. I planned on knockin' on the window to talk to him, but he drove off before I got there."

"And no one else knows anything about him?"

"Betty and Jerry don't. I talked to them a few times about it. I was plannin' to ask you about it when you got back, but I ain't seen you at home in a few weeks. Your sister came by a couple of times and got your mail. How's she doin' these days?"

"She's great. Listen, is the car out there now?"

"Lemme get to the window." Bob grunted and huffed. "Yep. It's there."

"Can you see the tag number?"

"Lemme get my shoes on, and I'll go tell you. You think it's someone up to no good? I knew I should'a reported it."

"I'm not sure yet, but I need to find out."

A door opened and closed on Bob's end of the call. "Give me a sec. Okay. It's TXV17."

"Colorado?"

"No, Tennessee. Don't see many of those 'round here."

A car engine rumbled, and Bob cursed under his breath. "He just took off. Definitely suspicious."

"I'm on it. Thanks, Bob. And please don't engage if you see it there again."

"Ten-four. When you comin' back?"

"I'm not sure yet. Hopefully, soon."

Heath brushed the sweat from his brow as he disconnected the call with Bob. The car had to be a lead. He had Jeremiah on the line a second later.

"I need you to run a report on a tag number. I'm sending it now along with photos of a vehicle that has been parked near my house on and off since I've been gone. The first known sighting of it was December first."

"I'll call you back."

Heath checked every surveillance camera in and around his house. He didn't have many. Freedom wasn't overrun with crime, and he had no reason to be overly cautious with his own home the way he was at headquarters.

Claire stepped into the kitchen fanning her face. "It's hot in here. Looks like the cookies are almost done."

A new email popped up in Heath's inbox. He didn't breathe as he opened the report on the tag number.

The name wasn't familiar, but he began a rudimentary internet search for Braxton Peterson. On the first page of hits, one name stood out against every word on the screen.

Jeremy Peterson.

Every piece of the puzzle clicked into place. Knox had gotten his nickname from his hometown and his Southern accent. He'd had a younger brother, one Heath had met when he'd visited the hospital during Knox's month-long fight for his life after the explosion.

Bile burned Heath's throat. He was going to vomit as soon as his lungs started working again.

"Everything okay?"

Claire's words were muffled as if he were hearing them under water, and he couldn't make out their meaning.

Jeremiah picked up the call on the first ring. "Who is it?"

"Where's Adam?"

"The resort lodge."

"Get him here now."

"What should I tell him in the briefing?"

Claire stood frozen in the middle of the kitchen, listening intently to his side of the phone conversation. "He's not after Claire. He's after me."

17
___

CLAIRE

*I*t didn't make sense. Who would be after Heath? Why him?

Heath's grip on her arms was tight, breaking her confused daze.

"Listen, Claire. I have to get away from you. Adam is coming. He knows where everything is."

She gasped, desperate to pull in a full breath. "Don't leave. Please."

"I have to."

"We can face this together." The old fear was creeping back in, but the courage Heath had fostered in her these last few weeks remained. "Don't leave. We'll call the police. They can help."

The worry in his brown eyes fueled the alarm that always preceded her panic. "I have to get as far away from you as possible."

She gripped the thick material of his hoodie at his sides. "Don't leave. You said we're safe here."

His hands palmed her head on both sides, focusing her attention on the sincerity in his words. "Do you understand what I've done? I've turned your world upside down—again! I did this to you. I stole your safety. I failed to protect you."

She tried to shake her head, but his hands prevented the movement. "No. We thought someone was after me, and you dropped everything to help me. Whatever comes next, I want to be with you."

"I brought the danger to you."

"Danger is a part of life. I know that now. I wouldn't want to face it with anyone else."

Heath sighed. "You could have been living your life these last few weeks. My mistake stole that from you."

"I wasn't living my life before you came along. I was going through the motions. Don't you see. I wasn't living, but now I am."

Heath's expression was hardened to her pleas, and he was slipping away from her with every word she said. She'd been living in a colorless existence before Heath came into her life, and the vivid light he'd brought was fading with his urgency to leave.

"I have to go." Heath stepped around her, and her hold on his shirt slipped.

"Don't leave like this. Please."

Heath pulled his bag from the coat closet, stuffing things into it as he moved around her. In the kitchen, he shut down computers and shoved them into carrying bags.

"Heath, listen to me." Her pleas were empty, and helplessness settled around her. Heath had shut her out.

The perimeter alarm rang through the room, but only Claire looked up.

"It's Adam. He'll stay with you until we know Braxton doesn't intend to harm you too."

"Who is Braxton, and why is he after you?"

Heath rubbed a hand over his mouth and looked at the floor where his things were packed into three bags. "Something happened during my time with the Marines. People were hurt because of me. Braxton's brother was one of those people."

"He's mad because you hurt his brother?"

When Heath's gaze met hers, a chill ran down her spine. "He's dead. Because of me."

Someone had died because of Heath? It didn't make sense.

Heath pointed a finger at his chest. Guilt and sadness swirled in his eyes. "This is my fault."

"I don't understand, but—"

Adam barged in. "Jeremiah said the PD have a BOLO for the vehicle. No word yet."

"I'm bringing the AR-15 and a smoke grenade."

Heath opened the pantry and entered the weapons cache.

"Claire."

Adam was speaking to her, but she couldn't take her eyes off Heath. He was leaving, and her heart was burning in her chest. The bond they'd been building in peace was being torn apart.

"Claire, I promise you'll be safe," Adam said.

"What about him?" she asked.

"Heath can take care of himself. He has us behind him too."

She didn't understand what had happened, but it couldn't be as cut and dry as Heath had said. If someone had died because of him, she knew there was more to the story.

Heath stepped from the narrow passageway and closed the entrance behind him. "I'll keep you posted. Call me if anything happens here."

He stopped in front of her, and the anguish in his expression was her undoing. Her breaths came in short gasps, but she refused to let tears well in her eyes. There wouldn't be any more crying. She was stronger than that now.

"Adam will keep you safe."

Heath would never forgive himself for this. He'd put as much distance between them as possible, and the flicker of hope that she'd see him again was dying. She wanted to scream at him, beg him to stay, and tell him she loved him, but the words were stuck in her throat.

"Don't go." It was her last shot, but there wasn't an ounce of hope left that he would listen.

"I'll check in with you soon." His hand brushed down her arm and gripped her hand. Too soon, the contact was severed, and Heath walked out the door.

She sank into the chair at the kitchen table. Numbness covered her as the heartache set in. So much happiness had been ripped from her so quickly.

"Heath will be okay. He knows what he's doing."

Adam's words were meant to encourage her, but they fell flat. What Heath was doing was pulling away from her, leaving her brokenhearted and confused.

The perimeter alarm sounded, reminding her that Heath was moving farther and farther away from her with each passing second.

"That should be Heath."

A loud crash sounded outside, and Adam hurried to the control panel by the door and pressed a few buttons.

Claire barely heard his mumble, but his speedy phone call caused her to lift her head.

An agonizing minute later, he ended the call and tried again.

"Jere, we've got company, and Heath isn't answering. Get the PD here now."

"Who?" Claire stood. Adam was talking to the person on the phone, not her. "What was that noise? Heath's out there!"

Adam pressed buttons on the panel, and the scene on the screen changed. Another button changed it again.

"Who is it?" she asked again.

Adam made another call and continued pressing buttons on the screen. "That sedan just crossed the perimeter. I'm looking for Heath. That sounded like a car wreck."

Claire jerked the phone from Adam's hand and listened to the ring. "You've reached Heath Mitchell."

She disconnected the call. "Where is he?" panic gripped her throat, making her words high and filled with panic.

"Found him!"

Claire pushed closer to Adam's side so she could see the screen where he pointed. The black sedan was parked in the middle of the road not far from the cabin. The SUV Heath had been driving rested in a nearby ditch, crumpled and smoking, as a man got out of the car and headed toward it.

18

HEATH

*H*ow stupid. Stupid. Stupid. Stupid.

Heath gripped the steering wheel hard and twisted his hands over the leather. He welcomed the burning with the release of his anger.

It wasn't enough. He'd messed up again, and this time, he'd put Claire in danger. Walking away from her felt like ripping out a part of his insides, but what choice did he have?

What did Braxton want? He'd tried to run Heath over and shot at him. Did the guy just plan to kill him, get that revenge, and move on? It wasn't like he'd meant for Knox to die. They'd been friends and brothers—closer than blood. He'd never meant to hurt anyone. Heath would change everything if he could.

The sun was setting on the mountain as Heath

pulled out onto the main road. The slick curves prevented him from speeding away, mounting his irritation.

He spotted the black sedan as he rounded the first bend. He'd been in such a rush to get out of the cabin that he hadn't stopped to think that Braxton might follow Adam in. It was the first time someone had come up the mountain without breaking up their trail with a vehicle switch.

The car veered to the center of the road, leaving no room for Heath to pass. Neither of them could be going more than thirty-five miles per hour, but a head-on collision at any speed could be a death sentence.

In a split-second decision, Heath chose the ditch on the left over the oncoming car or the steep mountain side. The tires held traction for a moment before sliding off the pavement. The impact jarred every bone in Heath's body, throwing him into the middle console and then to the driver's side window as his vehicle crashed into the side of the mountain.

There was a moment of peace before the pain settled in, radiating and pulsing in every inch of his body. Confused and barely conscious, Heath lifted a hand to his head. Wet. Holding his hand in front of his face, the blur was enough to make out the blood.

His thoughts were foggy, and focus was fleeting. What was he doing here?

The first thought was danger, then everything clicked into place. He pushed through the pain to unbuckle his seatbelt. Now what?

A scraping and rustling sounded somewhere nearby, but he couldn't discern the direction.

The passenger door opened and someone leaned into the cab before Heath could get his bearings. Every movement was slow as if his body was trapped in thick mud.

"Got you now."

Everything was still blurry when the man gripped Heath's arm and jerked, pulling his shoulder from its socket.

White hot pain stabbed at his shoulder. He'd dislocated it before, but he didn't remember it like this. The sting came in waves as the man jerked the arm again and again, pulling Heath's entire body over the console and through the open door.

Heath fought the fog of confusion and pain. He'd lose consciousness soon, but he had to come up with a plan first. He tried to focus, but it was impossible to hold a thought for more than a second.

There was a moment of weightlessness when he thought he'd lost consciousness, but it was over too soon as the freezing, wet ground broke his fall. Every bone in his body vibrated in pain.

The man leaned over him, but he still couldn't make out the face.

"Does it hurt?"

The voice was familiar. Knox. But it wasn't Knox. Knox was dead.

His brother. That memory clicked into place.

The man leaned closer. "Good. My brother suffered for a month. You owe at least that."

So that was the plan? Torture. No way was he letting this guy take him without a fight.

"Get in the car. We've got places to be." Braxton jerked the dislocated arm again.

An involuntary cry bubbled into Heath's throat, but he swallowed it. He'd die before he let this guy have that satisfaction.

Think. Think. What did he bring with him? He had a few weapons, but he could barely see, much less aim.

Smoke grenade. He'd grabbed two from the weapons vault. One was clipped on his belt. The movement only added to the pain, but the grenade was easily accessible. Heath pulled the cap and tossed it behind him into the path the man was dragging him.

Smoke filled the air, and the man stopped, coughing and cursing.

"Freeze!"

Smoke covered everything, and he didn't know up from down.

"I said freeze!" It was Adam.

Someone else Heath had dragged into this mess.

Heath's arm and upper body fell, hitting the ground hard enough to jar the breath from his lungs. The instinctual gasp sucked the smoke into his throat. He rolled over, coughing and fighting for a breath.

A deafening shot fired, and Heath lay paralyzed. Had he been shot? Everything already hurt. Would he be able to discern the new pain?

Was it Adam? Please, Lord, not another brother.

Fire shot through Heath's arm as he pushed up onto his good side. The black of his smart watch stood out against the pale-gray smoke, and the answer clicked into place.

"Jere. Send help." He'd never been so thankful for voice recognition. He had no way of knowing if the text was received, but it was something to hold onto.

He pulled his injured shoulder back, but the arm was useless. The next step was pushing up onto his knees. He could use his good arm then. When he was upright, he grabbed at his belt. The first thing he touched was a pistol. Not that. Everything was still blurry.

His arm jerked again, and nausea surged. Bile burned his throat as he gritted his teeth.

His fingertips touched the cool metal of a switch-blade. He could make it work.

The dislocated arm jerked again, and he could

just make out Adam's dark-blue uniform in the haze. He had Braxton in a restraining hold, but he hadn't loosened his grip on Heath's injured arm.

Heath inhaled, but the smoke filled his mouth and throat, burning him from the inside out. He just needed enough energy to make one pass with the knife. On the count of three, he jerked his good arm up, slashing the knife toward the arm that held his.

A scream filled the air, and Heath hit the ground hard. This time, he scrambled to his feet to help Adam, who strained to keep his hold on Braxton.

The wails of police sirens were faint, but they had to be close. Adam wouldn't be able to hold onto Braxton if he kept thrashing.

Blue lights and sirens rounded the nearest curve. Heath wasn't sure if the smoke was fading or if his vision was clearing, but the strobing lights were impossibly bright.

Pain radiated from his head to his toes. The only thing louder than the sirens was Braxton's screaming.

"Freedom PD. Put your hands up!"

Two officers ran to Adam and Braxton while another headed for Heath.

"I can only lift one arm," Heath cried as the officer approached.

The officer shouted over his shoulder, "We need a medic over here!" It was Ty.

Heath pointed back toward the safe house. "Claire is at the cabin."

"Is she injured?"

"I hope not. Someone needs to check on her. Now."

Ty spoke into his radio before examining Heath. "Weapons?"

"The belt and my ankle." He stood still and gritted against the pain as Officer Riggs removed the weapons from the tactical belt and ankle holster. A paramedic ran toward them carrying a bag of supplies.

"What are your injuries?"

"Dislocated," Heath said pointing to the shoulder. "Probably a concussion. I think my right side is bruised."

Behind the paramedic, Braxton thrashed and railed at an officer while another spoke with Adam.

"Heath!" Claire's strained voice cut through the noise and chaos on the road.

She was running toward him on the dark road. He hadn't made it a quarter of a mile from the cabin before Braxton had met him head on.

Relief washed over him instantly before horror ran cold in his veins. Jerking his head back to the line of police vehicles, he searched for Jeremiah or Adam.

"Heath, are you okay?" Claire asked.

"I think I have a concussion." Exhaustion weighed heavy on him. It was the kind he couldn't fight—the kind he knew from years of brutal football tackles in high school.

Adam was beside him. "They're taking him in. I'm going with them."

Heath nodded and winced. His brain bounced and banged inside his head, pounding with every movement.

The paramedic guided him toward the gurney. "Sir, you need to lie down until we can assess you for further injuries."

He knew what was coming. A neck brace, an IV, and enough X-rays to light up his insides.

"Heath, let's go. I'll ride with you."

Every word Claire said had his throat constricting. He still hadn't processed what all he'd done to her. Everything they'd done and every care he had for her was covered in a dark cloud of mistakes. So much for all his attempts to protect her. He'd led her to danger instead.

Claire wrapped her hands around his uninjured arm. "Heath, I'm here. I'm not leaving you."

Why did it hurt so much when she said things like that? He wanted it to be real, but it couldn't be—not after everything he'd done.

Pete stepped up behind Claire. Heath's team

knew who to call when they needed all hands on deck.

"Can you take her to headquarters?" Heath asked.

"What?" Claire asked.

"Just for a little bit. I need to talk to the police and make sure Braxton wasn't working with someone else."

"Okay." Her voice was soft and defeated, choking Heath again.

"Sorry, but I have to ride with him," Ty said. "It's protocol."

"Okay." Her whisper was carried away with the wind.

Every inch of his body hurt, but the ripping in his chest was the worst. He'd failed Claire when she needed him most.

"I'll be there soon." She twisted her fingers together. "Will you let me know where they take you?"

"I'll be out soon. Pete can get your parents to headquarters. They can stay with you until we can confirm Braxton was alone."

Claire bit her lips, but it didn't hide the trembling of her chin.

If they were lucky, the danger was over. Unfortunately, it also looked like the happy relationship he'd started with Claire was ending. He'd really screwed this one up.

"Jeremiah will refund all of your payments. He can do it as soon as you get to headquarters."

Claire brushed a hand over his arm. "I don't care about that right now. I care about you. It's over. Why do I feel like you're trying to get away from me?"

"I'm not. I just—"

"Sir, we need to get an IV started. You could have internal bleeding."

Heath held up a finger, indicating he needed a second. "I'll see you soon. Pete, take care of her."

"Yes, sir." Pete's usual smile was strained. No doubt he was waiting to give Heath a lecture about something. He'd failed everyone lately.

He hated seeing her like this. He wanted to go to her, wrap her in his arms, and tell her everything was going to be okay, but he didn't believe it himself. He couldn't lie to her.

He loved her. He loved her so much it hurt.

Stepping to her side, he brushed the side of his pinky finger against her hand. She linked her fingers with his and released a shaky breath.

"I'll be there soon. Pete can take care of anything you need right now."

"Okay."

He released her hand and met the paramedics near the ambulance.

Nothing was okay.

*P*ete parked in the Got Your Six headquarters garage. Save for his lone attempt to chat, the ride had been silent. Throwing open the car door, Claire shouted over her shoulder, "I'm going to the restroom."

"I'll be in Heath's office."

Poor Pete. None of this was his fault, but she couldn't stomach his optimism right now. He'd said Heath would be okay. He'd said Heath would come around. He'd said Heath would need some time.

Lies. She could hear it in Pete's chipper tone. He probably believed it, but she knew better. Well, she didn't know anything right now, and that's why she was furious. Holding it in on the ride with Pete had been miserable.

As soon as the heavy bathroom door closed, she

leaned her back against it, covered her face with her hands, and screamed. She wanted to be with Heath, but he'd put up an invisible wall between them. He'd dismantled years of her fears only to add a hefty load of heartbreak to the top.

When her throat was raw, her hands slid down her face and fell to her sides. She caught a glimpse of herself in the mirror. Red, puffy eyes told the story of the last few hours—the short time when everything had changed.

She took her time washing her hands, allowing the redness in her face to subside.

"Claire!" Her mother's call was tinged with concern.

"I'm in the restroom, Mom."

Her mother burst through the door. The comfort of the embrace brought on a new surge of fear. Was this really the end of what she'd been growing with Heath?

"I missed you," Claire whispered.

"I missed you too, sweetie. I'm so glad you're okay. Heath called us."

Claire raised her head. "He did?"

"He said you were safe and explained a little. I can't believe that man was after Heath the whole time. I'm just so glad it's over."

"Did he say anything else?"

Claire's mother rubbed a rhythmic circle on her

back. "He said he's refunding the money we paid." Her mother sighed. "I'm just so glad it's over."

Claire stepped out of her mom's arms. "I need to talk to Pete."

"He's in Heath's office with your dad. I still can't believe Pete helps out here. He just seems like your average Joe, and I'm finding out that what Heath and these guys do isn't average at all."

"I know. It's a little surreal."

As happy as she was to see her parents, her first priority was getting to Heath. Pete had brought her here under Heath's instruction, but she wasn't in the mood to obey his orders right now.

Pete and her dad wore smiles and joked in loud voices when she stepped into the office. Everything about the scene felt out of place.

"Hey, sweetie!" Her dad stood and wrapped her in a hug. "It's good to see your face."

"You too." She had missed them, but she'd been content and happy these last few weeks with Heath. "Have you heard anything else?"

Pete tapped on his phone. "Officer Riggs said they're pretty sure Braxton was working alone. Heath texted and said he's still waiting to be taken for x-rays."

"Can I go to the hospital now?"

Pete didn't answer. His gaze flicked to her parents.

"Why don't we give him some space?" her dad suggested. "I was just talking to Pete about a few legal matters. It seems Heath is concerned we'll sue."

Claire grabbed her dad's wrist. "You won't."

Her dad waved a hand. "Of course not. I got a good laugh out of it and signed a release."

Her shoulders relaxed. "Thank you. He didn't mean for any of this to happen."

"We know." Her mom rested a hand on her shoulder. "You've said nothing but good things about Heath since you met him. We believe he wouldn't have purposefully put you in danger. You've made some big steps these last few weeks."

"We don't want to mess that up for you," her dad added.

"I think you're too late. I'm afraid Heath has already ended things." She inhaled through the tightening of her throat. "And I'm okay. I promise I'm fine. I just need to see him."

"Heath won't forget this easily," Pete said. "But I think you can get through to him. He's humiliated that this happened on his watch. He would never want any harm to come to you, and then—"

"I know. And he thinks this was all his fault, but it wasn't. Even if we hadn't gone to the safe house together, that man would have come after him, and I would have still wanted to be with him through everything."

Her dad wrapped an arm around her shoulders. "Now that it's over, I can say I'm proud of you. I can't be so certain that I would have liked it had I known all of this from the beginning." He cleared his throat, fighting tears. "You're my little girl, and I never want you to be in harm's way, but you were so brave."

"I'll always be careful, but I'll be safer with Heath."

"We know this is important to you, sweetie," her mom said. "If you need to go see him, we understand."

A metal door clanged down the hallway, and Tessa shouted, "Claire!"

"In Heath's office!"

Tessa stormed in looking like she'd just rolled out of bed. "What happened? Are you okay? I got this cryptic and uninformative text from Heath to come check on you."

"I'm fine. I'm not so sure about him."

"Did he leave you? What has gotten into him?"

"It's a long story. Can you drive me to the hospital?"

Tessa's gaze traveled from Claire's head to her feet. "Are you hurt?"

"No. It's Heath. He was injured, and I need to see him."

"Which hospital?" Tessa asked.

Pete coughed. "Martin County Veteran's Memorial."

"Thanks." Tessa smiled at the ever-helpful Pete. "Hey, Mr. and Mrs. Odom. It's good to see you, but we have to run."

"You two go on," Claire's dad said as he shooed them out the door. "Tell Heath we're praying for him."

Claire wrapped her dad in a tight hug. "Thank you. I love you so much." She moved to her mom, who was still shedding a few tears. "Love you too. I'll call you soon."

"Be careful!" her mom shouted as Claire and Tessa raced to the garage.

Tessa pointed a finger at Claire. "You have a lot of talking to do."

"I'll talk. You drive."

*N*umbed by the IV pain meds, Heath dozed in the tiny emergency room. He'd gotten a private room with a small Christmas tree on a table in the corner, which seemed like a small blessing he didn't deserve. The shuffling and groaning of the nurses and other patients might have distracted him from his guilt.

Tessa burst through the tiny door with a smile on her face. "Hey!"

Tessa would lecture him about Claire, and that was the last thing he wanted right now.

Claire timidly stepped into the room behind his sister, and he stood corrected. The last thing he wanted to do was face Claire.

Coward.

"Bye!" Tessa waved as she walked back out the door, closing it quickly behind her.

Claire twisted her fingers around each other. She stood near the doorway as if a speedy escape might be necessary. He would never hurt her. At least not on purpose. She had to know that.

Heath gritted his teeth as he shifted in the bed.

"Are you in a lot of pain?" Claire asked.

"No. They gave me something for pain a few minutes ago."

She took a step closer. "What did the doctor say?"

"Broken rib, dislocated shoulder, and a mild concussion."

Claire looked at the floor. "I'm sorry."

"Why? None of this is your fault." The guilt pains surged through him again.

She jerked her gaze up to him. "You're right. It's that man's fault. Why would he want to hurt you?"

"His brother died because of me."

Claire interrupted. "How?"

"I gave the all clear on a building that wasn't."

"Why?"

"Because one of the other units said it was clear."

"So, it was your job to relay that message?"

"Yes."

"And you did that. You were the middle man, and you did your job as you'd been taught."

Heath sighed and winced. The pain meds were

doing their job. He'd forgotten about the sore shoulder and tried to move. "It's not that simple."

"Really? Because that's the way Tessa explained it, and it seems pretty clear that it wasn't your fault."

"You can look at it that way, but I said a word and two men died within seconds."

"What does that have to do with the man who came after you?"

"He lost his brother. Then he lost his job and his wife."

"Sounds like he was desperate and angry."

"He was, but I don't blame him. I might go crazy, too, if I lost one of my sisters."

Claire's chin shook for a moment before she tightened her jaw and straightened her shoulders. "I'm so glad you're okay, and I'm sorry."

"None of this is your fault," he repeated. "It's mine."

Her hands fisted at her sides. "It is not!" The surge of anger from Claire was new. She hadn't spoken a harsh word or raised her voice in the last three weeks.

"It's my fault for dragging you into this mess. I messed up so many times." He brushed a hand over his face and gritted his teeth against a wince. "The last thing I ever wanted to do was hurt you."

Claire was beside his bed in an instant, cradling his hand in both of hers. "Listen to me. You didn't hurt me. You changed me. You inspired me. You showed me I could be brave. Now, I want to show you how brave I can be. I want to weather this beside you."

"This is my—"

"If you say that one more time—"

Heath held up a hand. "Listen. What happened to you wasn't your fault. But me? This *was* my fault. I made a big mistake that cost people their lives. I could have cost you yours too. That's not a risk I'm willing to take. Ever."

"They caught the guy," Claire said.

"I deserved this."

"You deserve forgiveness," Claire said, her voice strong and final.

Heath shook his head. "Maybe, but not today."

"You're just afraid."

Fear. That's what this ripping was inside of him. "You're right."

"Didn't you tell me to let my faith be bigger than my fear?"

She didn't give an inch as she threw his words back at him. The timid woman he'd met almost a month ago was gone, replaced by a spitfire beside his bed who demanded he see things her way.

"Claire, I can't forgive myself for putting you in danger."

"I don't care," she spat. "I forgave you."

He shook his head. "It doesn't work like that."

"Yes, it does. I want to walk through anything and everything with you in this world. Good, bad, and dangerous."

It hurt. Words hurt. Now he knew why it was called heartache. His chest literally hurt without any physical injury.

She leaned closer and held his gaze. "You showed me how to face my fears, but it was all for nothing. The only thing I'm afraid of now is losing you, and I can't stop it from happening."

The choking in her words reflected the constricting of his throat. He loved her so deeply and purely, yet he couldn't be what was best for her. She deserved the safety and security of a quiet life, and he'd taken that from her from day one.

"I think you should go." He didn't want to say it, but he needed to. She needed to forget about him and what he'd cost her these last few weeks. She'd been scared enough, and he'd dragged her into the middle of more fear and uncertainty.

Claire stood, lifting her chin. "I'll go, but I'm not giving up. You were patient with me, and I'll do the same for you. I can't forget everything we said and did in that cabin. I won't. It was real, and I... I know what I feel, and it has nothing to do with that man or what happened in the past."

There were no tears on her face now, just bold

determination. Her resolve kindled a fire inside him, and he remembered the first time he saw her, the first time she fell into his arms, and the moment he knew he loved her.

All those moments began to burn, slipping away as she walked out the door without a backward glance.

21

CLAIRE

*C*laire had never jerked a door open before, and she certainly didn't think doing it in public was appropriate. Yet the wooden door to Heath's room in the emergency department banged into the wall beside it as she left.

She stormed down the short hallway to the waiting room and halted. All of her built-up anger demanded she continue stomping and fuming, but she didn't want to leave while Heath was still here.

Tessa stood and quickly tossed the magazine she'd been reading aside. "What happened?"

It seemed the answer was written on Claire's face. "I still don't know."

"I'm sorry." Tessa's arms were around Claire in an instant, leaving the shoulder to cry on all too accessible.

"He's putting this distance between us, and it's like I can't reach him. He's not listening at all."

Tessa squeezed the hug tighter. "This is all happening fast. Maybe you both need some time to process."

Heath needed time, but Claire didn't. Every second she left Heath with his thoughts gave him more time to talk himself out of the new relationship they'd been building.

"You'll get through this," Tessa whispered. "I won't leave you."

Claire heard the words her friend didn't say— that Heath might not come around—and she knew things were just as bad as she'd feared. Was he really calling this their ending when they'd just begun? She'd trusted him with everything. She'd given him the most fragile part of herself—her heart.

Now, she didn't have her own heart or his, and there wasn't anything that could have protected her from this hurt.

Tessa put her hands on Claire's shoulders and pulled back. "Buck up, buttercup. You're going to be just fine."

Claire squeezed her eyes closed, trying to hold the tears in. "Yeah."

"You've come so far. Don't let that bonehead set you back."

Claire chuckled and wiped her eyes. "He's not a

bonehead."

"You're right. He usually isn't, but I think he qualifies right now. It's just that I know he's thinking about all of this and how it plays into his relationship with you, his business, and basically his whole life. He's worked so hard to get past what happened when he was a Marine, and this is kind of a trigger for him. He made a mistake because he's human, and he doesn't allow himself much room for error. He's always been like that, even before those men died."

Claire sniffed and looked around for a box of tissues. "I know all of that. I'm just afraid he won't let this go."

Tessa grabbed for a tissue on a table near a Christmas tree and handed it to Claire. "I told you the answer. It's time. Both of you need it. And while you're waiting, don't forget how sweet he is."

Claire wiped her eyes and blew her nose. "He is sweet."

"Except when he's not."

"Whose side are you on?"

"Sorry. I'm a little ticked at him too right now."

Claire's shoulders slumped. "I'm tired."

"You've been up all night. Let's go."

"I can't leave him here."

"Mom and Dad are on their way," Tessa assured as she nudged Claire toward the exit.

"Let's stay until they get here then. I don't want

something to happen while no one is here for him."

Tessa squeezed Claire's hand. "You're a good one, you know that?"

"Right now I feel like a loser, so maybe don't ask how I feel about myself for a while."

Tessa plopped down in a chair. "Help me with this crossword. It's all stuff about the American Revolution, and I suck at history."

The night she'd met Heath, Claire had a feeling her life was about to change. And it did. She'd felt the shift in the air, in her life, and in her heart. After a few weeks with him, she'd changed into someone who knew what it was like to love and be loved in return by Heath Mitchell.

Now, she knew what it was like to lose him.

HEATH SHOVED the white blankets around on the hospital bed and searched the small emergency room for anything that belonged to him. The PD had taken all of his weapons, and it left him with the feeling he was missing something.

"Mom, have you seen my—"

"Right here." She held up his wallet—the only thing he'd brought with him. He'd even left the vehicle key with Jeremiah who was handling the towing.

"I hate that you got up in the middle of the night to run over here. I told you I'm really okay."

"Hush and put your shoes on." His mother pointed to his socked feet. "Hospital floors are filthy."

"Yes, ma'am." He sat on the side of the bed and shoved his feet into his boots. It had been a long time since he'd stayed up all night like this, and he needed a bed—any bed except this one. "Is Tessa here?"

"No, she left to take Claire home just a minute ago. She said she'd meet us at the house."

"Claire?"

"No. Tessa," his mother said.

Of course Claire wanted to get home. Of course she didn't want to see him. He'd sent her away like a jerk. He'd regretted the words as soon as they were out of his mouth. He'd been stupid to think she'd stick around after all he'd put her through.

"You can call Claire when we get on the road. She's been a nervous wreck."

"She has?" Heath asked. "Was she in the waiting room this whole time?" He checked his watch. "It's morning."

"She was worried. Tessa said she'd stay with Claire for a bit before coming home."

"That's good. Thanks for the ride, but I wish you'd let me call one of the guys."

His mom shoved the discharge papers at him.

"Nonsense. What are mothers for?"

He wrapped his uninjured arm around his mom. The other shoulder had been set back into the socket, but he'd be in a sling for a while.

The ride home was anything but silent, and there was no way he'd be calling Claire with his mom right beside him. What would he even say to her? He might be able to squeeze some info about Claire out of his sister when she got home.

When his mother passed the turn to his house, Heath sat up straighter. "You can take me home. I promise I'm fine."

"Not until I feed you. You haven't had anything to eat in at least twelve hours." Her attention stayed focused on the road.

Trying to convince her to take him home was a lost cause. He rested his head back against the seat. Sleeping on his parents' couch wasn't ideal, but he'd take what he could get right now.

The house was quiet when Heath and his mom entered. His dad was at work, and Tessa was probably still with Claire. The Christmas lights and decorations contrasted with his gloomy mood.

"You get settled, and I'll be back in a bit. Bacon, eggs, and toast?"

"Sounds good. Thanks." Heath winced as he eased onto the couch. Whatever relief the hospital meds had given was wearing off.

"Breakfast is ready!"

Heath jolted from his light sleep and sucked a breath through his teeth. He'd need to ice the shoulder after breakfast.

The front door slammed, and he craned his neck over the couch. Tessa stomped into the living room and threw her purse onto the recliner.

When she stood in front of him, she propped her fists on her hips. Was she trying to look angry? Her furrowed brow resembled one of those fuzzy ankle-biter dogs that yipped a lot.

"Have you lost your mind?" she shouted.

"I don't think so. It's pounding enough that I know it's still in my skull."

"Claire is devastated!"

Heath's head fell back. "I'm sorry."

"Your apologies are no good here. Action is necessary." She stomped a foot and pointed at the floor.

"I can't change what happened." The realization was all too real, and something he wasn't prepared to think about until he'd gotten at least a few hours of sleep.

"You can sure fix it. I set the two of you up, and now you're being a jerk to my friend. Besides that, your actions reflect poorly on me. I told her you were a great guy!"

Heath swallowed. Tessa was madder than a wet cat, and he hated letting her down. That seemed to be the trend for the last few weeks. He'd failed Claire, her parents, and his team at Got Your Six when he'd wasted those weeks at the safe house chasing the wrong lead.

But they weren't wasted weeks. They were great weeks spent with Claire. At least until he found out about the mess he'd made. Now that cloud of failure hung over every memory.

Tessa's shoulders slouched, and she sank onto the couch beside him. "I love you, but you're being awful to my friend."

"I don't want to do that. I wanted—"

Tessa held up a hand. "Don't tell me what you wanted. Tell me what you want. Then go after it. I know the two of you can be happy together. I know you like her. She likes you."

"I love her." The words were out before he'd given them a second thought. It was a truth as tangible as his bones.

Tessa gasped. "Does she know that?"

Heath shook his head.

"You have to tell her."

"How? I'm a grade-A loser. I thought I was protecting her, but I was really putting her in danger."

Tessa rested her hand on his. "Listen to me carefully." She held his gaze without blinking and whispered, "You're being stupid."

"Gee, thanks."

"It's tough love, but someone has to say it. I can also try Spanish or Italian if you don't understand."

Heath huffed and rested his head back. The pounding was growing stronger.

"You know what Claire needed? Assurance. Confidence. Loyalty. Bravery. Courage. She has all of those things now." Tessa held up a hand. "Notice I didn't say she needed *you* or *a man* or *love*. She needed to believe in herself. I don't know how you did it, but you made her see how strong she could be. No one else has been able to get through to her."

"She *is* strong." He knew why it was hard for Claire to see it, but he believed in her.

"Now she knows. And you've left her heartbroken when she finally decided to open up to you. Jerk!" Tessa slapped Heath's arm.

"Watch it. That's the one that dislocated."

"I know. I wanted you to feel it."

Heath hung his head. "I guess I deserve that."

"Now that we've established right and wrong, I need you to implement the solution to this problem."

"How?" he asked

"I don't know. I haven't gotten that far. But I nailed the lecture, didn't I?"

Heath wrapped an arm around his sister's shoulders. "You did. Maybe you should be a motivational speaker."

Tessa perked up. "Really?"

"No. I was joking. Don't quit your day job."

"Speaking of jobs—"

"I'm not hiring you," Heath interrupted.

"That's not what I was going to say. Pete offered me a job, and I took it. You're looking at the new secretary at O'Rourke Rentals."

"Fantastic. You think you'll like it?"

"I don't know, but he's going to show me all about the cabins. I think I might like being in the tourist industry."

"Meet new people every day? That sounds right up your alley."

"Right? This might be my thing."

"You're a great sister and friend. I think that's your thing—being a good person."

"Aww. You're so sweet." She wrapped her arms around him and squeezed.

"Ahh!"

"Sorry!" Tessa slapped both hands over her mouth.

"I need food and a nap."

Tessa extended a hand to help him off the couch. "Then you'll go to Claire's and make up?"

"Maybe tomorrow. I have an idea, but I need time to think it through."

22

CLAIRE

*B*eing able to paint in her home studio again was both relieving and upsetting. She'd enjoyed painting at the safe house with Heath in the next room, and she missed him. Everything reminded her of him—the faint smoky smell of a fireplace, the numbers in the code for the security system, cooking meals she now had to eat alone. So much had changed in the last few weeks. Her home wasn't familiar anymore.

Adam had dropped off the rest of her things last night, and she had just finished putting the final touches on the second Freedom Lake series. Julia at the Art and Soul gallery had gone on and on about the first paintings.

Claire rested her brush in the cleaning solution. A cloud of sadness had followed her since she got home. It was stupid. She shouldn't be so heartbroken over a man, but Heath was different.

The ringtone for her dad played the chipper whistling of *the Andy Griffith Show* theme song. She stood and wiped her hands on a rag. She needed to stop staring at this painting, but the possibility of hearing her parents' pleas to stay with them again made her hesitate before answering.

"Hello."

"Hey, sweetie. I have bad news."

"What?" How could her dad throw those words around? And with an upbeat tone. What was wrong with him?

"Nothing to worry about. I just can't make our hike this week."

Claire's shoulders sank. Their hike was the only thing she'd been looking forward to since she got home. They hadn't been out together in weeks. "Why?"

Someone knocked on the front door. She barely heard it from her studio at the back of the house.

"I got a call," her dad said. "Something came up."

"Okay." She shouldn't be upset. Her dad was an adult with many responsibilities. Still, it wasn't like him to cancel their hike unless something important needed his attention.

The knocking sounded again.

"Do you need to get that?" her dad asked.

Claire pulled the phone away from her ear and stared at it before replacing it. "How did you hear that?"

"Talk to you later, sweetie. Love you."

"Love you, too." Why was her dad rushing her off the phone?

She made her way through the house, peeking out every window. How disappointing that she'd fallen back to square one where the mail lady could send her into a panic attack.

She lifted onto her toes to peek out the tiny viewer window in the door. It was Heath.

Claire disarmed the security system and threw the door open. He looked strong and healthy, aside from the blue sling that cradled his arm. His smile was only half-hearted, but it sent a tickling up from her toes just the same.

"Hey." He scratched his head and took a deep breath.

Claire still hadn't caught her own breath.

When she didn't reply, he cleared his throat. "I talked to your dad. If you're wondering why he said he couldn't hike with you today, that's because of me."

She still couldn't inhale. Heath was here, and she had no idea what to say.

"I asked him if it would be okay if I offered to go with you. You can tell me to get lost so you can go with your dad if you want. I just figured I'd need a lot of time for this big apology I have planned."

"Yes." The word rushed out of her throat. "Yes, I want to go with you."

Heath's shoulders sagged in relief. "Good. I know you're not happy with me, but I want to do everything I can to change that." He reached for her hand and clasped it. "I messed up. More than once. I put you in danger, but then I let you down when you needed me. I was ashamed, and I feel awful for everything I put you through."

Short, quick breaths flitted into her lungs. Tears were close behind. Her emotions had been upside down and backwards these last few weeks, but the roller coaster was coming to a stop.

Heath looked down at their linked hand, then back up. "I love you. I love you so much I can't think straight. I'm sorry for hurting you. I'm sorry for making you second guess how much you mean to me. I hope one day you can forgive—"

"I do," she interrupted. "I already did. I love you too."

Heath's arm wrapped around her. Careful not to touch the arm resting in the sling, she laid her cheek on his chest and tightened her arms around his middle.

"I'm not mad at you," she said. "I know why you've been struggling with this. Tessa told me everything, and I get it. I know why this was so hard for you. But you can trust me. I'll stand beside you through your happiness and doubts. Even knowing the danger, I would choose to stay with you every time. And if you ever feel like you've failed or messed up, know that you're not alone. You're human, and so am I. I just don't want to go through life without you by my side."

Heath hugged her tighter. "I love you."

Claire lifted her head and grinned through her tears. "I love you too."

He wiped at the tears on her face before cradling her cheek and pressing his lips to hers. That breath she'd been chasing since he'd shown up at her door flooded into her body like water filling a dry valley.

When they broke the kiss, the tears were gone, replaced by a wide smile.

"Freedom Lake?" she asked.

"Today. Next time, I want to see something new with you. I want to see everything with you and watch you paint the things we see and bring them to life again."

That was an offer she couldn't refuse.

23

HEATH

*C*laire squeezed Heath's hand. "Stop fidgeting. Everything is fine."

"Easy for you to say. I'll probably stay at the top of your dad's watch list until the end of time."

She chuckled, and the joyful sound rolled over his skin, leaving a tingling in its wake.

"No such thing. Dad is the most mild-mannered man I've ever met."

Heath parked his SUV in front of her parents' house and brushed his hand through his hair. It was a nervous habit. One he hated because it had gotten him in trouble in uniform. "I want them to like me. I mean, I want them to *really* like me."

Claire leaned over the console and pressed her lips to his cheek. The spark that lingered could have rivaled a live wire.

"I love you, and they will too."

He slid his hand behind her neck and pulled her in. When she said things like that, he lost any ability to fight the urge to kiss her. Claire's kisses were soft and slow with a hidden intensity that kept him up at night.

Unfortunately, it would reflect poorly on him if her parents decided to look out the window right now.

He broke the kiss and rested his forehead against hers. "I love you."

"Let's go in. My mom has only called twice in the last hour asking where we are."

Claire didn't wait for him to come around and open her door. Right now, he couldn't blame her. These were frostbite temps, and he wanted to get inside just as much as she did.

Her mom met them at the door with a smile and a hug. "Merry Christmas Eve!"

Heath's stomach spoke up when the smell of apple pie reached him. Had Claire told her mom it was his favorite?

"Merry Christmas Eve." Claire looked around the house. "Where's Dad?"

"Back deck."

"Why? Does he have a death wish?" Claire asked.

"He insisted we deep fry the turkey. Please act

like you're at least impressed by his attempt, even if it tastes horrible."

Heath rested a hand on Claire's shoulder. "I'll go see if he needs any help." Anything to move dinner along so he could get to that apple pie.

Claire's mom clasped her hands. "Good. I could use a hand with the potato salad."

He almost felt bad for offering his help when he saw Claire's exaggerated pouty lip. Leaning in, he whispered, "Don't worry. I'll be on my best behavior, and I'll come find you soon."

"Promise?" She winked, sending his pulse into overdrive.

He definitely wanted to take back his offer to help with the turkey. If someone had told him six weeks ago he'd be so hung up on a woman that he would be reluctant to leave her to tend a deep fryer, he'd have laughed them out of Colorado. Yet that's where he stood—thoroughly in love with a woman who'd flipped his world upside down.

On the back deck, Claire's dad was pulling the turkey out of the hot grease. Holding it awkwardly, he jerked his head toward the nearby table. "Can you get that for me?"

Heath grabbed the large pan and held it under the turkey.

"Whew. That thing is bigger than I thought." Mr. Odom wiped at cold sweat on his brow.

"I'm here to help."

Mr. Odom clapped a hand on Heath's shoulder. "I know. And you've done that. My Claire is happier than I've seen her in years. I didn't think she'd ever get over what happened, but it looks like you've done it."

Every mention of what happened to Claire in college made his stomach roll, but he swallowed the sick feeling. "It wasn't me. It was her. All in the Lord's timing."

Mr. Odom shook his head. "I love her more than anything. I hope your intentions are good. She's my baby girl."

The "intentions" talk. Heath should have seen this coming. "I promise my intentions are good—the best."

"It's Christmas Eve, and things seem to be going well with you two. I know the happiness of the holiday can seem like a good time to—" Mr. Odom waved his hands in the air.

"I'm not planning on proposing."

The older man's shoulders relaxed. "Thank goodness. I support the two of you one hundred percent, but—"

"It's too soon. I know that. I fully intend to ask her to be my wife, but I'm a patient man."

Mr. Odom wiped at his eye. "You're a good one, son."

Was the air getting thicker? Heath sucked in the freezing wind, trying to calm the thoughts that were pushing to the forefront of his mind. Did her dad know he had a ring at home? He'd left it in a drawer in his bedroom because he'd been too tempted to bring it with him tonight. Claire had some kind of magical effect on him that turned off his brain and made him want to do crazy things, like propose to her after a month of dating.

Claire needed a slow-growing relationship, and her dad's concerns affirmed Heath's earlier decision to wait. He'd bought her Christmas gift with that patience in mind. If she wore his necklace for half a year, maybe she'd agree to wear his ring.

Claire

TESSA BARRELED out the side door of her parents' house before Heath had shifted into park.

"Let me see!" Tessa screamed while she was still ten feet away.

Claire lifted her chin as her boots crunched in the snowy driveway. Apparently, the happy tears she'd shed at her parents' house when Heath gave her the gift were going to make an appearance again.

Tessa gasped as she inspected the necklace in the glow of the colorful Christmas lights. "It's gorgeous!"

"Did you help him pick it out?"

Tessa shot a slanted stare at her brother. "No. He wouldn't let me."

Claire brushed her fingertips over the oval sapphire. The blue stone was so dark, it looked black against her white scarf. The midnight blue was her favorite color, and now she'd be able to wear it around and see it every time she looked in the mirror.

"You did good, bro." Tessa barreled into Heath with arms wide open.

"I did well," he corrected. "Superman does good."

"Ha! Good thing I'm not planning to be an English teacher." Tessa grabbed Claire's hand. "Let's go."

Claire giggled as she tried to keep pace with Tessa without falling on her backside in the slushy snow. How was it possible to be this happy? Spending a quiet, peaceful Christmas Eve with Heath's family as well as her own seemed like the kind of far-fetched dream she'd never thought to pray for before now. Yet, God had blessed her beyond measure. Her old, simple prayers seemed laughable in the wake of what God was capable of giving.

Inside, Heath's parents were quick to welcome her, and she met Cora and Rachel for the first time. They were as friendly as the rest of the Mitchell family.

Since Claire and Heath had eaten dinner with her family, they settled down with everyone in the large, homey living room to open gifts. She rubbed her fingertips over the pendant on her necklace as Heath's dad stood and prayed.

"Lord, thank You for allowing all of us to come together to celebrate the birth of the Savior tonight. Thank You for the many blessings You give us daily, but today we're especially thankful for our loving family and Jesus Christ. We pray that You would go with us for another year and help us to be a light in the world as we worship You. Amen."

Tessa jumped to her feet and started handing out gifts. Claire opened her gift from Heath at her parents' house earlier, but she'd sent Heath's gift with Tessa a few days ago. He'd know what it was as soon as he saw the shape, and she wanted it to be at least a little surprise.

Tessa swung around with the rectangular canvas wrapped in red-and-gold paper. "This one's for you." She handed it to her brother with a wink.

"From Claire," he read.

"Did you think she didn't get you anything?" Tessa joked.

"No, I just didn't think about it."

Tessa clapped a hand on her brother's shoulder. "Nice one, bro."

He tore open the paper and rested the bottom of the canvas on his knees.

"What is it?" Cora asked.

Claire waited for Heath's reaction, but his expression revealed nothing as he studied the painting. When she'd held her breath long enough that her lungs were sore, his mouth turned up at the edges.

"It's a painting."

"Thank you, Captain Obvious," Tessa said. "Show us."

He turned it around to reveal the scene from Freedom Lake where they'd sat and eaten lunch the first time they'd hiked together.

"It's beautiful," his mother said. "I have a few of your others hanging in the hallway. You have a wonderful talent, Claire."

"I think that's my favorite ever," Tessa said.

Holding the canvas in front of his face, Heath gave her a look that said he knew this wasn't just any painting. It was special to them. What he didn't know was that the painting captured the moment she'd realized she could trust him with her heart.

EPILOGUE

Heath
Six Months Later

*M*r. Odom raised his glass of sparkling grape juice to Heath from across the room. Heath waved him over. The Art and Soul Gallery was packed shoulder-to-shoulder for the showing, and Heath was guarding his spot against the rear wall. He'd already chatted with everyone and didn't want to get lost in the crowd again.

"How is she doing?" Mr. Odom asked as he pushed his way out of the crowd to where Heath waited.

"She's all smiles. I saw Tessa a few minutes ago, and she said there are only three paintings left."

"You're serious?"

"Did you expect anything less?" Heath kept his hands in his pockets and fought the urge to tug at his tie. He was used to wearing dress blues, but his tux fit tight in all the wrong places, despite the alterations. "Our friends support her, and they all want a C. Odom original hanging on their wall."

Mr. Odom said as he scanned the faces. "Is Loraine with her?"

Claire's mom had been by her daughter's side all evening, gushing and smiling as patrons, friends, and family oohed and aahed over Claire's most anticipated series. Heath tipped his champagne flute toward Claire and her mother.

Claire's dad made a humming noise in his throat. "I sure am proud of her."

"You have good reason to be. She has a gift. And look at all these people." Heath's family and all of his and Claire's friends were here tonight, except Aiden and Joanna who stayed home with their son, Landon, who had a summer cold.

"Just think how happy she'll be later." Her dad nudged Heath's shoulder.

"I hope so." He'd been trying not to think about the ring in his pocket, but he wasn't having any luck. He'd been turning it with his fingertips all evening.

"I'm not worried about it."

Heath pushed up the cuff of his sleeve. "I need to find my parents and Tessa. It's almost time."

"Glad I made it," her dad said.

"I wouldn't do this without you."

Her dad leaned around him. "I see them over there with Pete."

Heath and Mr. Odom joined his parents, Tessa, and Pete near the refreshment table where he hoped Tessa wouldn't spoil the surprise with her giddy smile. Heath whispered to his family when he got the text from Julia asking if he was ready.

The owner of the Art and Soul Gallery stepped onto the small platform, and the chatting fell to whisperings as Heath made his way to the front of the room.

"Good evening, ladies and gentlemen. Thank you for coming to the C. Odom exhibit tonight. We're blessed to have such amazing talent in our small town. Claire has been sharing her gift with locals and tourists for years, and it was time we recognized her and the gift of her fantastic paintings."

Everyone applauded, and a few of Claire's friends cheered and whistled. Heath took his place beside Claire whose smile beamed.

"I've asked Claire's boyfriend, Heath Mitchell, to give us a special introduction before we hear a few words from our artist."

Heath squeezed Claire's hand and stepped onto the low platform. "Good evening. I want to thank everyone for showing your support for Claire tonight. She's a fantastic artist, but she's also a friend to many of us. If you don't know her, I can promise you that she paints these canvases with her whole heart. She has a way of seeing the beauty in the world like no one else."

He caught sight of Tessa in the crowd and almost lost his nerve as a tear raced down his sister's cheek. She wiped it away so quickly, he questioned whether he'd actually seen it.

Clearing his throat, he turned to Claire and held out his hand. "Claire, can you come on up?"

Another round of applause filled the room, matching the racing of his pounding heart. Her hair was pulled up into a bun of curls and her dress was a sparkling midnight blue that matched the necklace she wore, but her smile was bigger and brighter than he'd ever seen.

"Claire, you're a light in the life of everyone you encounter." Heath knelt on a shaky knee, bringing the microphone with him.

Claire gasped, and their friends and family did the same. He knew she wanted to marry him, or he wouldn't be putting himself out there like this. He could have proposed in private, but he wanted

Claire to be surrounded by a room full of people who loved her.

"Will you marry me?" He'd had a long speech planned, but he couldn't think of a single word past the four most important.

Claire whispered, "yes." Then she grabbed the microphone from Heath. "Yes! I said yes!"

Heath stood and wrapped her in his arms. Their friends and family cheered, but he still heard Claire's soft words in his ear.

"I love you."

"I love you too."

Ready to find out more about Officer Ty Riggs? Return to Freedom Ridge in Trusting the Hero, the eighth book in the Heroes of Freedom Ridge series.

Join in all the fun at our Facebook Group for sneak peeks, giveaways, and tons or Christmas romance fun!

HEROES OF FREEDOM RIDGE

Heroes of Freedom Ridge Series

(Year 1)

Rescued by the Hero (Aiden and Joanna)
Mandi Blake

Love Pact with the Hero (Jeremiah and Haven)
Liwen Y. Ho

(Year 2)

Healing the Hero (Daniel and Ashley)
Elle E. Kay

Persuaded by the Hero (Bryce and Sabrina)
Elle E. Kay

Romanced by the Hero (Mac and Amy)
Liwen Y. Ho

OTHER BOOKS BY MANDI BLAKE

Blackwater Ranch Series

Complete Christian romance series

Remembering the Cowboy

Charmed by the Cowboy

Mistaking the Cowboy

Protected by the Cowboy

Keeping the Cowboy

Redeeming the Cowboy

Wolf Creek Ranch Series

Truth is a Whisper

Unfailing Love Series

Complete small-town Christian romance series

Just as I Am

Never Say Goodbye

Living Hope

Beautiful Storm

All the Stars

What if I Loved You

The Blushing Brides Series

Multi-author series

The Billionaire's Destined Bride

The Heroes of Freedom Ridge Series

Multi-author series

Rescued by the Hero

Guarded by the Hero

ABOUT THE AUTHOR

Mandi Blake was born and raised in Alabama where she lives with her husband and daughter, but her southern heart loves to travel. Reading has been her favorite hobby for as long as she can remember, but writing is her passion. She loves a good happily ever after in her sweet Christian romance books and loves to see her characters' relationships grow closer to God and each other.

CONNECT WITH MANDI

WEBSITE | AMAZON | FACEBOOK
INSTAGRAM | GOODREADS | NEWSLETTER

ACKNOWLEDGMENTS

First, I want to thank Tara Grace Ericson for bringing this series together. The Freedom Ridge series has been a blessing in so many ways, but I'm especially thankful for the friends I've made. Hannah, Liwen, Elle, and Jessie are the best authors to work with, but it doesn't feel like work when we're having this much fun.

Thank you to everyone who helped make this book better. Pam Humphrey, Tanya Smith, Jenna Eleam, and the Freedom Ridge authors all chipped in their advice and suggestions. I also owe a thanks to my advanced readers who always catch those last few typos.

Thanks again to Brandi Aquino for her editing skills and Amanda Walker for designing a beautiful cover for all of my books.

I'm incredibly blessed with friends and readers like you who support me. Thank you for taking a chance on this book. I hope you enjoyed reading it as much as I enjoyed writing it.